THE HOBBIT

AN UNEXPECTED JOURNEY

OFFICIAL MOVIE GUIDE

THE HOBBIT™
AN UNEXPECTED JOURNEY

OFFICIAL MOVIE GUIDE

BRIAN SIBLEY

Houghton Mifflin Harcourt

Boston   New York

2012

CONTENTS

'The question was: "Who are we going to get to direct this movie?" I guess it was at that point that I began to rethink whether or not I could take it on. In the end, I said to myself: "If I *were* going to make a film of *The Hobbit* then it would have to be a film that I wanted to see and one I could enjoy directing." I then had to decide how I could make that process enjoyable and finally made the decision that I was going to be the same filmmaker I had been on *The Lord of the Rings* but was simply returning to Middle-earth to tell a new story.'

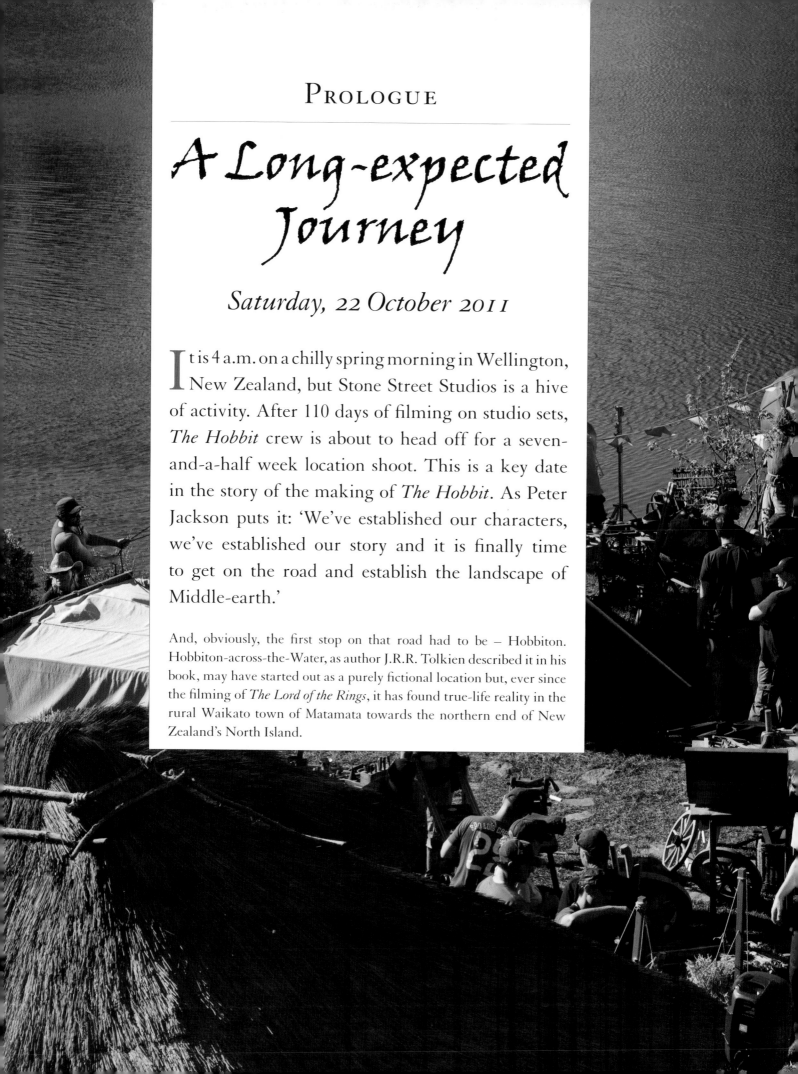

PROLOGUE

A Long-expected Journey

Saturday, 22 October 2011

It is 4 a.m. on a chilly spring morning in Wellington, New Zealand, but Stone Street Studios is a hive of activity. After 110 days of filming on studio sets, *The Hobbit* crew is about to head off for a seven-and-a-half week location shoot. This is a key date in the story of the making of *The Hobbit*. As Peter Jackson puts it: 'We've established our characters, we've established our story and it is finally time to get on the road and establish the landscape of Middle-earth.'

And, obviously, the first stop on that road had to be – Hobbiton. Hobbiton-across-the-Water, as author J.R.R. Tolkien described it in his book, may have started out as a purely fictional location but, ever since the filming of *The Lord of the Rings*, it has found true-life reality in the rural Waikato town of Matamata towards the northern end of New Zealand's North Island.

Driving into Matamata you pass a sign that reads 'Welcome to Hobbiton', and since the global success of the *Rings* trilogy hundreds of visitors every day have found their way to the town and to the 1,250 acre area of farmland chosen by Peter Jackson in 1998 as the first key location for his epic film project.

For a decade, the abandoned remnants of Bag End, home to Bilbo and Frodo Baggins, and the other hobbit holes of Hobbiton, have proved a popular tourist destination for fans who want to get as close as possible to places where *Rings* was filmed. Yet for the past two years this iconic location has been undergoing a massive renovation to return it to its original detailed and landscaped perfection, ready for some of the opening scenes in the new movie.

The distance by road from Wellington to Matamata is just over 340 miles. It would take about six and a half hours to drive there by car, but Transport Manager, Glenn Shaw, is allowing eight hours for the fleet of trucks that is about to head off into the pre-dawn darkness.

Mr Bilbo Baggins may have set out from Bag End on an *un*expected journey, but for Glenn today's expedition to Hobbiton is a *long-expected* journey: the culmination of months of planning and coping with what he proudly describes as 'the biggest logistical move in cinematic history'. But as time ran out and the day drew closer, it seemed more like 'a constant rolling nightmare'.

'Essentially,' says Glenn, 'everything comes on wheels. Everybody operates out of their vehicles: Camera Department, Props, Costumes, Prosthetics, Hair and Make-up. In addition, there are 500 crew members and everything they need: catering facilities, generators for electricity, supplies of water, portable toilets and all the computers

and office equipment necessary for people to carry on with their jobs while they are away on location.'

There is such a vast amount of equipment that it will take almost 140 trucks to move everything needed by the film's Main Unit from Wellington to Matamata and beyond. Put all those vehicles end to end and they'd take up getting on for a mile. Incidentally, these figures do not include a further 60 trucks and 200 crew members required by the Second Unit, which is also taking to the road.

'It was a full-time job,' says Glenn, as the first of the vehicles pulls away, 'just finding enough trucks and drivers for the convoy. And since most of those drivers will have no knowledge of the work to be done by people operating in or out of the trucks, we have a team who will be respon-

'IT IS A JOURNEY MOVIE AND, IN THIS CASE, AN EPIC JOURNEY; THAT'S WHY IT IS CRITICAL WE SEE THE CHARACTERS TRAVELLING THROUGH POWERFUL SCENERY. ALSO THERE ARE MANY SCENES INSIDE ROOMS, CAVES AND UNDERGROUND TUNNELS THAT CAN GET QUITE CLAUSTROPHOBIC.'

sible for arranging everything: connecting utilities – water, power, communications systems – and having everything up and running within an eight-hour turnaround so that filming can start as soon as the cast and crew arrive on location.'

As filming comes to an end at Hobbiton, that team will then set off, ahead of everyone else, to get preparations underway at the next location. It's a demanding job, working round the clock and through the night: the tasks remain the same from place to place, all that changes is where they are being done and whatever local problems come with them – whether that's being halfway up a mountain or in an almost inaccessible river gorge.

So, where do you put all those trucks when they arrive? Supervising Locations Manager, Jared Connon, who joins us, has the answer. 'Very large fields! Whenever we look at a location we have to make sure that it's possible to fit everything into the space that's available. And we need a *lot* of available space, the equivalent, in fact, of three rugby pitches: one for parking, one for the facility vehicles and one for the equipment trucks.'

With 140 vehicles driving around and people tramping on them, it doesn't take long – especially if it rains – for those rugby pitch-sized fields to turn to mud. 'If there's sufficient time,' Jared explains, 'we will do earthworks and put down gravel and road metal to create bases for the incoming vehicles. But we have to weigh up the expense of making those preparations against how long we are going to be on site.

PREVIOUS: *The Production transforms farmland just outside Matamata into a hobbit market just outside the* Green Dragon Inn. OPPOSITE: *Dwarf masks worn by the actors' doubles are carefully checked to ensure they survived the journey intact.* ABOVE: *Stone Street Studios at dawn.* OVERLEAF: *Director Peter Jackson discusses the next scene with Martin Freeman as the crew stands ready.*

Sometimes it's better to spend the money before you arrive, sometimes after you leave. There is no point in spending 100,000 New Zealand dollars building a parking facility for one day when you can fix up the mess afterwards for 50,000!'

Today's activity, though a mammoth undertaking, is just the beginning. Tomorrow, the cast and crew will be flying up to Hamilton, where over 200 rental cars will be waiting in the airport car park for the final stage of their journey to Matamata. In the midst of a stressful piece of strategic planning, Glenn Shaw is grateful for one thing: had the Rugby World Cup not ended a week ago it would have been even harder to access all the cars required.

The trucks keep rolling by, laden with cameras and sound equipment, wet weather protection, heaters in case it turns cold; there are truckloads of swords, axes, bows and arrows, artificial trees and a small garden of real plants, Dwarf wigs, beards and body-suits and prosthetic hobbit ears and feet, not to mention miscellaneous livestock (49 sheep, 15 chickens, 9 goats, 5 steers, 4 pheasants, 2 ducks and a pig) and 60 kilos of toilet paper.

Location filming involves a vast amount of work, so why is it considered such an essential dimension to Peter Jackson's vision of Middle-earth?

For Glenn, the answer is simple: 'It is a journey movie and, in this case, an epic journey; that's why it is critical we see the characters travelling through powerful scenery. Also there are many scenes inside rooms, caves and underground tunnels that can get quite claustrophobic. Location shots open up the film and allow the audience to feel that they can breathe.'

Jared agrees: 'One of the things that won the fans over in *The Lord of the Rings* was the unbelievable vistas and scenery. They were magnificent and Peter naturally wants to shoot bigger and better location shots for *The Hobbit* than were seen in *Rings*. The locations we have chosen are very special because they will seem, to the rest of the world, to have a very *otherworldly* look; a slightly off-kilter appearance that should make you feel you are seeing the kinds of mountains or woods you have never seen before.'

It is now 8 a.m. and the last of the trucks is passing through the gates of Stone Street Studios. Jared and Glenn will shortly be heading off to Wellington airport to fly to Hamilton from where they will drive to meet the convoy as it arrives at their first destination.

That long-expected journey has begun…

Professor Tolkien & Mr Baggins

J.R.R. Tolkien's *The Lord of the Rings* has been described as the 'legacy' of his earlier book, *The Hobbit*, so it is fitting that Peter Jackson – having already transferred that legacy onto film as a hugely successful movie trilogy – should now return to Tolkien's realm of Middle-earth in order to bring *The Hobbit* to the cinema screen.

But how did this tale of thirteen Dwarves, a hobbit, a wizard and a dragon come to be written?

It was in 1930 that John Ronald Reuel Tolkien, Professor of Anglo-Saxon at Pembroke College, Oxford University, was engaged in the tedious job of marking exam papers. To his great delight, he came across a sheet of paper which one of the candidates had left blank. What could be more welcome to the weary professor than a page that *didn't* require marking? However, it was at this moment that, suddenly

– unbidden and out of nowhere – a curious sentence came into Tolkien's head. Despite having no idea what the words meant, he wrote them down: 'In a hole in the ground there lived a hobbit...'

It was a while before Tolkien found the time to decide what a 'hobbit' was, eventually describing them as a race of little people, about half the height of a human. 'They dress in bright colours,' he wrote, 'wear no shoes, because their feet grow natural leathery soles and thick warm brown hair like the stuff on their heads (which is curly); have long clever brown fingers, good-natured faces, and laugh deep fruity laughs (especially after dinner, which they have twice a day when they can get it).'

Tolkien developed the character of this hobbit living in a hole in the ground and an adventure began to unfold. A story of how Mr Bilbo Baggins, a well-to-do hobbit of Bag End in the Shire, finds himself caught up in a hazardous quest to the Lonely Mountain in an attempt to help a company of Dwarves recover treasure stolen from them by a dragon named Smaug.

Along the way, Mr Baggins and his companions encounter Trolls, Elves, Goblins, giant spiders (Tolkien was an arachnophobe, having been bitten by a tarantula when he was a child in South Africa), a skin-changer who can transform himself from a man into a huge bear, and 'a small, slimy creature … as dark as darkness' called Gollum who owns a very precious thing – a magic ring that gives the wearer the power of invisibility.

The story went through numerous revisions and name-changes: the wizard Gandalf was originally called 'Bladorthin' while the leader of the Dwarves, whom we now know as Thorin, was at first named 'Gandalf'!

As the manuscript grew, Tolkien told the story to his children as an after-tea serial during winter evenings. It was also read by several of Tolkien's Oxford friends, among them the man who would later create the Land of Narnia, C.S. Lewis, and, by a series of chances, came to the attention of the publishers George Allen and Unwin, who encouraged the author to complete the book.

When, in October 1936, Chairman Stanley Unwin received the finished typescript, he asked his ten-year-old son, Rayner, to write a report on it. 'This book,' wrote the young reviewer, '…is good and should appeal to all children between the ages of 5 and 9.' Rayner was paid one shilling for his appraisal of a book that has since become an international bestseller! With maps and illustrations by the author, *The Hobbit, or There and Back Again* was published in 1937.

The Hobbit sold out its first print run of 1,500 copies in three months and the reviews were highly appreciative, with W.H. Auden calling it 'one of the best children's stories of this century' and C.S. Lewis describing it as having 'a fund of humour, an understanding of children, and a happy fusion of the scholar's with the poet's grasp of mythology'. No wonder the publishers were soon asking the author for 'another book about the Hobbit'.

Twenty years earlier, Tolkien had begun to write what he called *The Book of Lost Tales*. These writings that would later become known as *The Silmarillion* took the form of an epic fantasy – equalling the great mythologies of the world – centred on a realm known as Middle-earth.

It gradually became clear to Tolkien that 'the world into which Mr Baggins strayed' in *The Hobbit* was, in fact, Middle-earth and this realization influenced the way in which he began writing his sequel. Bilbo's original exploits proved to be but a prologue to a far more mature and complex saga that, over a decade-and-a-half later, would be published in three parts as *The Lord of the Rings*.

The Hobbit has continued to be a widely read and much loved book, both for itself and as a prelude to Tolkien's later masterwork. As a result it has been much interpreted in a variety of forms: newly illustrated by several artists, read as an audio book, dramatized for radio and adapted for the stage, but it would be seventy-five years before a feature-length version of Bilbo Baggins' journey there and back again would come to the screen.

From The Lord of the Rings to The Hobbit

'I've given up worrying about trying to influence things too much. A film director has to take on so much responsibility and control that I quite like letting some of it go. There are times when you just have to put your hands up and leave things to sort themselves out.'

Peter Jackson is talking about the lengthy and often fraught journey that would eventually lead to his filming *The Hobbit*.

It was a journey that began on Wellington railway station in 1978, when seventeen-year-old Peter Jackson bought a copy of another of Tolkien's books – the one-volume paperback edition of *The Lord of the Rings* – as something to read during a twelve-hour train ride to Auckland, where he would be studying for a job as an apprentice photoengraver.

The book had cover art from the recently released animated film directed by Ralph Bakshi. Peter had seen the film and – like many others – found it rather bewildering, not least because it stopped halfway through Tolkien's story. Perhaps reading the book might help resolve some of the confusion.

'Being mad about movies,' recalls Peter, 'and being fascinated by the whole business of filmmaking – and, in particular,

special effects – I kept saying to myself, "This book could make a really great movie!" Of course, it never even occurred to me that *I* could make it – I didn't even fantasize about making it! That would have been ridiculous. But I *did* think, "I can't wait for somebody to make a full-blown, live-action film of *The Lord of the Rings* – because I really want to see it!" Years later, I came to the conclusion that – since nobody else seemed to be going to be doing that – I would simply have to make it myself! But that was way off in the future.'

That future eventually arrived in 1995, by which time Peter was an established filmmaker whose sixth picture, *The Frighteners*, was in post-production. The possibilities allowed by advances in the computer effects that were being used on that film triggered a conversation about future project ideas between Peter and his partner, Fran Walsh: 'I said, "What's not been done well for a long time is the fantasy genre like a *Lord of the Rings*-type story." That felt like the kind of world that I'd want to create as long as it could be very *real*: amazing buildings and creatures, but real environments, characters and emotions; a story that is relatively serious with depth and complexity and where nothing would look artificial or fake.'

Impossible though the prospect sounded, enquiries were made and it was discovered that film rights to both *The Lord of the Rings* and *The Hobbit* were owned by Saul Zaentz, producer of such films as *One Flew Over the Cuckoo's Nest*, *Amadeus* and *The Mosquito Coast*. That discovery led to four tortuous years during which time several major studios became involved (and then *un*involved) with a project that began life as a deal for one film adapted from *The Hobbit* followed by two from *The Lord of the Rings*, before shifting (when rights to *The Hobbit* proved difficult to secure) to two films solely based on *Rings*. In the face of rising budgets,

that option was subsequently downsized to *one* film before, miraculously, being re-born as the trilogy that eventually began filming on Monday, 11 October 1999.

Once *The Lord of the Rings* secured its reputation as a multi-Oscar-winning juggernaut of a blockbuster, the inevitable speculation swiftly began as to whether *The Hobbit* might now also be filmed. The complex rights situation meant that the films would eventually be made by New Line Cinema and Metro-Goldwyn-Mayer and distributed by Warner Bros, but that situation was only reached after a further six-year saga of negotiations, lawsuits and any number of unforeseen glitches and delays.

What was widely known from the earliest stages of the project was that Peter Jackson was not keen on the idea of directing a prequel to *Rings*. 'Let me tell you,' says Screenwriter and Co-Producer, Philippa Boyens, 'Pete had absolutely no intention of directing this movie. He really didn't. He was incredibly happy to let somebody else do it. I truly think it was easier for Pete to let it go than it was for

somebody else to come in, take on the project and try to re-create what was already so clearly and fully defined.'

Looking back on his initial decision, Peter says, 'I imagined that, if I were to make these films, I would be frustrated because I would be constantly thinking about what I had done on *The Lord of the Rings*. I would somehow feel that I had to build or improve on that. I thought it would be a fairly unsatisfying experience to have to compete against my own movies.'

In 2008, Mexican-born director, Guillermo del Toro – responsible for such idiosyncratic movies as *Cronos*, *Mimic*, *The Devil's Backbone*, *Pan's Labyrinth* and the *Hellboy* franchise – was engaged as director.

Collaborating via videoconferences and on flying visits from Los Angeles to New Zealand, Guillermo joined the *Rings* team of Peter Jackson, Fran Walsh and Philippa Boyens on the task of structuring and writing the screenplays. He also began working on design concepts with a number of artists, including Alan Lee and John Howe who had contributed so much to the look of the earlier films.

OPPOSITE: *The production would visit some remote but beautiful locations in its quest to portray new vistas in Middle-earth.*
ABOVE: *Peter steps back into Bag End in one of* The Hobbit's *earliest marketing images.*

Richard Taylor and his team at Weta Workshop were already re-immersed in the world of Middle-earth. 'We had done three years of *pre*-pre-development before anyone was helming the film,' recalls Richard, 'and had produced a sizable body of work through sheer enthusiasm and stupidity! Then Guillermo came on board and we had a magnificent time collaborating with this dynamic, crazy, wonderful person.'

'I KEPT SAYING TO MYSELF, "THIS BOOK COULD MAKE A REALLY GREAT MOVIE!" OF COURSE, IT NEVER EVEN OCCURED TO ME THAT *I* COULD MAKE IT!'

Despite such positive achievements, progress was slower than had been anticipated and by 2010 *The Hobbit* had still to be officially 'green-lit'. The creative delays were compounded by financial difficulties at MGM and, at the end of May 2010, Guillermo del Toro withdrew from the project.

'Guillermo was sad to leave,' says Peter, 'and we were sad to see him go. For us he had been a very exciting choice and to have seen Middle-earth through a new filmmaker's sensibility would have been very interesting, but MGM's financial problems meant that the deal between them and Warner Bros couldn't close. It was out of everybody's hands and fate decided that it just wasn't to be.'

In fact, even after Guillermo's departure, the project remained in abeyance for several further months. The names of various directors were rumoured as possibly taking over the project, but in October 2010 it was announced – as many fans had long hoped – that *The Hobbit* would now be directed by Peter Jackson.

Recalling that period, Philippa Boyens says: 'By the time it became clear that Guillermo wasn't going to direct, I think Pete had become so involved in the writing and the creation of the world that it felt a lot easier to take on the task than he probably originally imagined.' Discussing the circumstances that led to his taking up the reins, Peter says, 'When Guillermo had to leave the movie, the question was: "Who are we going to get to direct this movie?" I guess it was at that point that I began to rethink whether or not I could take it on. In the end, I said to myself: "If I *were* going to make a film of *The Hobbit* then it would have to be a film that I wanted to see and one I could enjoy directing." I then had to decide how I could make that process enjoyable and finally

made the decision that I was going to be the same filmmaker I had been on *The Lord of the Rings* but was simply returning to Middle-earth to tell a new story.'

Even after the confirmation that Peter was going to be back in the director's chair, further delay ensued as a result of an industrial dispute involving various actor's unions, as well as concerns relating to interpretation of New Zealand labour laws, both of which created a distinct possibility that the films would have to be shot outside of New Zealand. That eventuality was averted after a series of negotiations with the New Zealand government and the production was set to begin filming in New Zealand at the start of 2011, with the release of *The Hobbit: An Unexpected Journey* scheduled for December 2012 and *The Hobbit: There and Back Again* to be released the following year.

Yet another hiatus followed when, at the beginning of 2011, Peter was admitted to hospital with a perforated stomach ulcer and the press was once again wild with speculation over the future of the project. Despite excitable media talk of 'The curse of *The Hobbit*', the team soldiered on with preparations and on 21 March 2011, with Peter out of hospital and recovered, principal photography finally began.

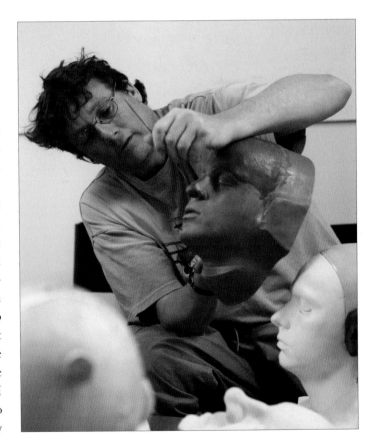

OPPOSITE: *(Above) Peter, Carolynne Cunningham and Phil McLaren enjoy the view from Bag End. (Below) Welcome to Middle-earth!* ABOVE: *Richard Taylor.*

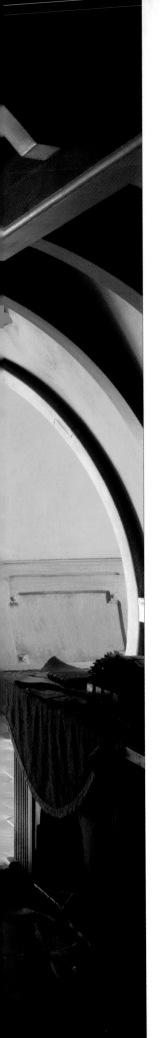

Opening the Door to Bag End

'We'd like a picture of the hall in Bag End with the door standing open and a view of the landscape beyond. *Just* the open door and the view – *no Hobbit!*' That was the request which John Howe received from HarperCollins*Publishers* in 1995 when they were preparing to publish the book, *The Map of Tolkien's The Hobbit*.

It was one of the many publications that Peter Jackson amassed when planning first began on *The Lord of the Rings* trilogy; when John Howe started work on the conceptual designs for the film, Peter told him that this cover art was exactly the look he wanted for the movie version of Bag End.

'Despite the fact that Peter is such an original character,' says John, 'who thinks in such disconcertingly innovative terms most of the time, he doesn't insist on imposing something new where he recognizes that something already in existence is in line with his vision. His reaction to the Bag End painting was very gratifying because I knew I had the licence to build on something that belonged to me. I could develop it with integrity and honesty, responding to the subject as I'd instinctively responded when I did the original illustration. In the nicest way, such moments are something you hang on to as you move along through this vast project that has a life of its own.'

ABOVE: *John Howe's famous painting,* A Hobbit Dwelling, *was a clear inspiration to the filmmakers* (OPPOSITE), *though the door now opens the other way.*

Jackson Returns to Middle-earth

'It was really only unexpected circumstances that put me back in the driver's seat. But, having ended up there, I'm really enjoying myself.'

Peter Jackson has just completed filming a sequence in which a gathering of hobbits, old and young, are celebrating 'an event of special magnificence', as Bilbo might say. The young hobbits – many of them children of the cast and crew – have OOHed and AHed as Peter repeatedly yells *'BANG!'* and studio lights flash to simulate Gandalf's fireworks that will, eventually, be seen exploding above the Party Field in Hobbiton.

'*The Hobbit*,' says Peter during a break between takes, 'is more episodic than *Rings* which, in *The Two Towers* and *The Return of the King*, had several different storylines that could be intercut. So we looked beyond the pages of the novel and into Tolkien's Appendices to *The Lord of the Rings*, which tell of events leading up to and following those narrated in *The Hobbit*. Using this material has helped us take the story into Tolkien's broader mythology.'

Peter was also aware that Tolkien had decided to revise *The Hobbit* in 1960, twenty-three years after the book's first publication. His aim had been to bring it into line with what he now understood about the history of Middle-earth from having written *The Lord of the Rings* and to change the tone to one that was closer to it. After three chapters, however, the revision was abandoned as being too much of a change to a book that was already known and loved.

'In our adaptation of *The Hobbit*,' says Peter, 'we have done something that Tolkien didn't succeed in doing in print and, hopefully, this will come fresh to people who will have never seen the full story playing out in chronological order.'

The difference in tone that had concerned Tolkien, between the adventures of Bilbo and the journey undertaken by Frodo, had been one of the reasons why Peter was initially reluctant to direct the new films: 'For a long time

ABOVE: *Peter Jackson, the Wizard of Wellington.* OPPOSITE: *Ian McKellen, standing on a box, proves that Gandalf knows how to party, especially when he has brought fireworks to entertain the hobbits.*

I had thought of *The Hobbit* as a children's book and *The Lord of the Rings* as being more adult. *Rings* is about a dramatic confrontation between good and evil that builds to an apocalyptic conclusion. *The Hobbit* is simply about a group of Dwarves who are trying to regain their homeland – it is not the fate of the world that's at stake. Because of that, I felt that going back into that world to make a film for a younger age group was something I really didn't want to do. I had to find a way into it and the way I've done that is through the characters of the Dwarves.'

The trouble was that, for Peter, the Dwarves were also a cause for apprehension: 'Frankly, I was a bit nervous about the idea of thirteen Gimlis! It was the ultimate ensemble and very scary: all those Dwarves, a hobbit *and* a wizard; fifteen central characters who have to share the screen. We had coped with nine in *The Fellowship of the Ring*, until the breaking of the Fellowship, but here we were facing the same number of characters – *plus an additional six!*'

The solution, as Peter goes on to explain, was to define those thirteen characters: 'We needed to know what type of Dwarves they were, so we began by listing their heritage, background and position in society, from members of the Dwarf royal family to working class.'

Screenwriter Philippa Boyens, who has been watching the filming of the hobbit party scene, describes the next stage: 'We had Thorin as leader and around him we established a series of distinctive family groups: Balin and Dwalin, old warriors and members of the nobility; Fili and Kili, younger, eager and enthusiastic; Oin and Gloin, the well-to-do merchant class; Dori, Ori and Nori, middle class; and Bifur, Bofur and Bombur who were, we decided, miners from the west.'

These decisions provided plenty of potential for humour. 'Individual characters can offer humorous possibilities,' says Peter, 'but when you have a group you have a different dynamic. The Dwarves are rather like a union committee. Whenever they make decisions, they go into a huddle and almost take a vote!'

Clearly writing for so many characters, as individuals and as a Company, was a challenge. 'What we didn't want to do,' says Philippa, 'was overload the film with too much information upfront. When you read Tolkien's books you see that he reveals his characters gradually in the telling of the story so we tried to follow his lead. Rather than panic about having thirteen Dwarves and the audience needing to know all about them, we allowed them to become known to us as they become known to Bilbo.'

The characters were further refined as the actors were cast and began to inhabit their roles. 'Having fleshed out the characters,' says Peter, 'we wanted to cast really good, suitable actors who would be able to have fun in the parts. We wanted to make sure that some of the roles went to local actors because I have worked successfully with a number of them before and because we are intrinsically part of the New Zealand film industry. But whether they came from home or abroad, everybody who's in the movie won their right to be there.'

Peter also wanted to ensure that the various differences between the Dwarves' characters were reflected in their appearance: 'The design – make-up, hair, costume and props – were vitally important. We wanted to make them visually distinctive. You might think thirteen Dwarves would be confusing, but you eventually reach a stage where if you saw them all in silhouette, you'd be able to distinguish them one from another.'

Considerable thought was also given to the character of Bilbo. 'It was very hard,' recalls Philippa, 'because, at the beginning, your main character in the story is being swept along like a piece of luggage. But what you can't do is turn him into the hero hobbit. Bilbo can never take on that role. Every motivation in his character is an honest, genuine one. For example: he is brave in the Goblin tunnels not because he is a hero, but because he desperately wants to get out of there and survive. What is amazing about him – and it's something that is of great importance to the events that unfold in *The Lord of the Rings* – is that he does not kill Gollum in order to escape.'

It's time to resume shooting, and as Peter prepares to go back on set, he observes: 'I never dreamed I'd be back in Hobbiton with Gandalf or standing on the set of Rivendell with Elrond. We all came together a decade ago to make *The Lord of the Rings* and we did what we did: the actors created their roles and I filmed them. It was a period of time that has subsequently become part of popular culture. Back then they weren't established, instantly recognizable characters, but since we last worked together images of Ian McKellen as Gandalf, Cate Blanchett as Galadriel and Orlando Bloom as Legolas have adorned everything from magazine covers to lunch boxes all over the world. Ten years on, to suddenly be sharing a set with what are now iconic characters is a strange feeling. Of course, they didn't think they'd get to play those characters again any more than I thought I'd be directing them; so, although there was a time when I couldn't imagine myself doing this film, now I'm in the thick of it I'm really very pleased it's turned out this way.'

ABOVE: *Peter and Martin Freeman prepare for one of Bilbo's earliest scenes.*
OVERLEAF: *The journey begins!*

A Fresh Exploration of Middle-earth

'Each filmmaker has his own vision,' says Peter Jackson, talking about the first major challenge he faced on taking over the directing of *The Hobbit*. 'Guillermo del Toro had done a year's worth of work on the look of the film and a lot of it was terrific, but I couldn't inherit his designs. It's not an ego thing; I just thought it would be a terrible mistake to try to step into his boots and make a Guillermo del Toro film, because he's the only person who could do that. I decided I would need to go into my own imagination and make the movie I was seeing in my head.'

Major considerations resulted from that decision, as Weta Workshop's Richard Taylor recalls: 'Although we were very sad when Guillermo moved on, it meant that Peter would be helming the project and that was fantastic for us. Understandably he wanted to revisit the design process to reflect his own taste and aesthetic and this gave us a chance to re-envision everything from a standpoint that was complementary to our earlier shaping of the world in *The Lord of the Rings*. The one drawback was that Peter was unable to start until twelve weeks out from the first day of production; so, instead of the three-and-a-half years we had to prepare for *Rings*, we had just three months!'

With typical Kiwi can-do mentality, Richard was undaunted: 'This project is beyond our wildest dreams and the opportunity to work with Peter on revising the look of the film was invigorating. If you see tight deadlines as a curse, you can't develop. If you see them as a challenge then there is a level of excitement and fulfilment. At the end of the day, the work is the work; where you find satisfaction and enjoyment is in the people with whom you work.'

Richard's view of the collective creativity that *The Hobbit* represents is shared by the film's Production Designer, Dan Hennah: 'We don't work with anyone who is less than fabulous at what they do. We employ people who have their own imaginations and have something to contribute: artists, sculptors, designers and artisans in all kinds of crafts and trades – saddle-makers, glass-blowers, potters, jewellers and wooden-toy-makers – but they must still be able to accept that our task is to embrace Peter Jackson's vision and get that vision onto paper and then onto film.'

'Not only that,' adds Art Department Manager, Chris Hennah, 'they have to be the kind of people who, when asked, can do the seemingly impossible and do it to a standard that it is really impressive.'

For the Art Department, as for Weta Workshop, the deadlines have been testing: 'This time,' says Dan, 'things have been rather more frenetic with only months of pre-production work for a project that needed at least a year, but we have learned from the experience of having worked on *Rings*. We went into those films very naïvely in terms of understanding what Peter wanted to portray. Having had that practice we have been able to plan more efficiently.'

CLOCKWISE FROM TOP: *A beautifully detailed hobbit market outside the* Green Dragon Inn, *with The Mill in the distance. Standby Painter Genevieve Cooper puts the finishing touches to a hobbit beer barrel. Gollum's coracle floats in his cave waiting for its master to return.*

Returning to Middle-earth has also provided the opportunity to revisit some of the settings created for *Rings* and to add some new embellishments, such as the White Council Chamber in Rivendell and, at Bag End, a previously unseen bedroom, dining room and pantry.

But, as Dan explains, *The Hobbit* has also opened up many new possibilities for the film's Art Department: 'This is a road movie and in travelling that road Bilbo and the Dwarves are discovering different and contrasting cultures. We have tried to reflect the epic nature of the journey while being true to our collective vision of Tolkien's world. It is essentially the same Middle-earth geography that we established in *The Lord of the Rings*, but whereas in those films we went south, this time we are going east. So, in terms of our world, the inspiration for these eastern locations would be Norway, Russia, even some Asian influence, although it is always just a suggestion rather than anything too specific.'

As with *Rings*, the intention is to give a resonance of the familiar and to help root Tolkien's fantasy realm in a believable reality, although with some of the settings in *The Hobbit*, such has the labyrinth of caves beneath the misty Mountains,

where the Goblins dwell, it is their very sense of unfamiliarity that makes them so striking.

The process by which this 'Goblin Town' and the other sets in the film were created began with talks between Peter and Dan, invariably in company with the film's Conceptual Art Directors, Alan Lee and John Howe.

'All the time we're talking,' says Dan, 'Alan and John are drawing and coming up with amazing concepts, every one of which has epic potential. They understand Peter's language; they know what is going to delight him, and how to capture his vision. They have brought to *The Hobbit* their unrivalled knowledge of Middle-earth and their flair for making something that could be quite ordinary into something utterly spectacular.'

'We show Peter our initial drawings,' says John, 'and see which direction he wants to take. He'll usually go through them making two piles: one of images that he finds interesting and one that he doesn't feel are relevant. The stack he is interested in then becomes our resource for the next version we work on. It is always a back and forth process because there's no telling which drawing is going to set something off in Peter's mind.'

ABOVE: *A detailed model by the Art Department of the climactic scene in the pine-trees is built as a full-size set* (INSET), *which when dressed is ready for filming.* TOP RIGHT: *A fully dressed Rivendell set, complete with telescope.* RIGHT: *Using detailed set plans, the set builders turn John and Alan's concept for Radagast's home, Rhosgobel, into a full-sized, timber-framed structure, which when painted and fully dressed* (FAR RIGHT) *is brought to three-dimensional life.*

As Alan notes, Peter will occasionally reference an image that one of them created for a book or a calendar, possibly years earlier: 'Peter has an extraordinary memory and even recalls pictures that we have forgotten! Sometimes we'll know what he's talking about, sometimes not, and there have been occasions when it's been easier to simply draw what he's described as remembering rather than try to find the original!'

'The time we spend with Peter,' says John, 'is very special. He is always excited by seeing new images and clearly likes working with us because we respond to his ideas, thoughts and reactions to what we've done.'

For John and Alan, despite many years of illustrating Tolkien's writing, *The Hobbit* has provided a chance to explore locations in Middle-earth that either they haven't previously had an opportunity to depict or, at least, not in the detail required for set design.

Alan is particularly pleased with the look that emerged for Dol Guldur (an Elvish name meaning 'Hill of Sorcery', which is referred to in *The Hobbit* and Tolkien's appendices to *The Lord of the Rings* and which figures in the films): 'It started out in early drawings as being a place created out of thorns but developed into a structure based on triangular shapes. I like using geometry and the good thing about using triangles is that they suit the camera eye very well, because you can take in most of the set with just a few camera moves; you get very good value from a triangular building because you're not

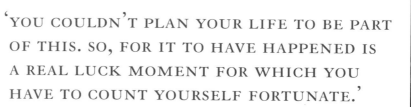

always losing detail in the corners. Each of the three sides to the courtyard has three niches – nine in all – and we added doorways with diamond-shaped tops, which was an idea we had toyed with for the Paths of the Dead sequence in *Rings* but not developed.'

For John, one of the sets he finds satisfying is the lair of the Goblins: 'Goblin Town is underground and, for the Dwarves, filled with potential danger. But, basically, it is a hole in a rock and there are not many things more boring than that! So what we did was lift this place off the ground and perch it in mid-air. The Goblins live in a world that is cantilevered out over a bottomless chasm on rickety structures that have been jerry-built from wall to wall by wedging old planks into cavities.'

'YOU COULDN'T PLAN YOUR LIFE TO BE PART OF THIS. SO, FOR IT TO HAVE HAPPENED IS A REAL LUCK MOMENT FOR WHICH YOU HAVE TO COUNT YOURSELF FORTUNATE.'

The Art Department turns in, on average, half-a-dozen concept drawings for Peter's consideration every day; and, because they are a way of viewing the bigger picture, they include both those parts of the set that will need to be built and those elements of the environments that will be added later by computer as what are called 'digital extensions'.

So, does Dan ever look at Alan and John's pencil drawings and wonder whether they can be convincingly created in reality? 'Well,' he replies, 'the first question is *how much* has to be physically created, and then how can we build it?'

Those questions are resolved by translating the concept drawings into set designs, with all the necessary measurements required by the set builders. Those technical drawings are then used to build physical scale models.

'For *The Lord of the Rings*,' says Dan, 'we built models on quite a simple scale, but now we are creating highly detailed models that not only show more of the building than Peter can *afford* to have built, but are bigger than he is going to require for the scenes he has to shoot. This provides the basis of a negotiation about what is needed and what can be afforded. It's all about answering two questions: why build less than you are going to need or more than you are ever going to see on screen? It's all about money, detail of design and our being able to get on and build sets without Peter needing to be involved in a continuous approval process.'

The models are discussed in relation to a detailed budget drawn up by a full-time estimator, who daily

monitors what is being planned and built. It is a fact that some sets that may not occupy a lot of screen time are, nevertheless, more important than others because, visually, they are of major significance to the storytelling. However, the Art Department's guiding principle is simple: 'We don't spend a penny more than we *have* to,' says Chris Hennah. '*And*,' adds Dan, 'we never spend a penny less than we *need* to!'

At the time of our conversation, the Art Department has produced a staggering ninety seven major set pieces, although that figure is somewhat misleading since, depending upon what mix of characters have to appear in those scenes, a set may have to be built to two different scales.

Because it isn't possible for everyone in the cast to be on call for eighteen months' filming, shooting schedules are constantly affected by actor availability. As a result, many sets are built, dismantled and later reconstructed. 'We keep everything,' says Chris, 'all the component parts of the set, every prop and every piece of decoration.'

Asked how long it takes to build a set, Dan has a swift response: 'It depends how much time we've got!' A huge set will generally require up to six weeks, although the various elements to the set are constructed elsewhere and then assembled in the studio prior to the start of filming. 'It takes a week to put a set together on a sound stage,' says Dan, 'but that actually represents *two* weeks' work because we use rolling crews of art directors, construction people, carpenters, fabricators, painters, decorators and finishers working twenty four hour shifts. We're careful how we schedule the work – welders obviously have to be kept away from painters using flammable paints – but we use every single hour of the day, and night, until the job is done.'

Having collaborated with Peter from *The Frighteners* via *The Lord of the Rings* and *King Kong* to, now, *The Hobbit*, Dan is impervious to the rigours of the tasks that he and his department daily face. His response is one that is shared by dozens of people involved in this extraordinary project: 'You couldn't plan your life to be part of this. So, for it to have happened is a real luck moment for which you have to count yourself fortunate.'

Top: *Not the most comfortable resting place. Under Peter's watchful eye, crew perfect a scene in Goblin Town, part of which can be seen below it in scale model form.*

MARTIN FREEMAN

The Hobbit with the Furrowed Brow

Bilbo Baggins is on the run. He is hurtling down a hillside, along with thirteen Dwarves, dodging between tall pine trees and he is looking rather worried. Small wonder, since Gandalf has just yelled that they are about to be attacked by Wargs.

It is another unexpected encounter on this unexpected journey that would alarm most people, let alone an unadventurous hobbit like Mr Baggins. Then, fortunately, Peter Jackson calls 'Cut!' and everyone breaks for lunch.

Sitting outside his trailer in the sunshine of a New Zealand spring day, Martin Freeman looks rather concerned. Not as much as Bilbo facing the Wargs, but definitely a bit anxious. This is not too surprising, since the furrowed brow is something of a Freeman trademark. Martin's BAFTA award-winning performance as Doctor John Watson in *Sherlock*, a TV drama series updating the detective stories of Arthur Conan Doyle, quite often finds him looking a bit perplexed. This natural ability to look worried is a useful asset in playing such an unlikely hero as Bilbo.

'That,' says Martin, 'is what makes it part of the stuff of a million stories, legends and myths; and that's something which people have always wanted to read and storytellers always wanted to tell: the idea of a transformation taking place within a character from the beginning to the end of the story.'

When it was first announced that *The Hobbit* was to go into production, people began telling Martin that he ought to play Bilbo but – not knowing the book at the time – he didn't give it too much thought.

Martin had played various dramatic and comedic roles on stage and screen before appearing as Tim Canterbury in the cult BBC comedy series, *The Office* with Ricky Gervais. Further TV series have alternated with feature films including Richard Curtis' *Love Actually* and

OPPOSITE: *Bilbo considers the journey ahead.* ABOVE: *Kili (Aidan Turner), Bilbo (Martin Freeman) and Bofur (James Nesbitt).* BELOW: *Peter frames the next shot.*

The Hitchhiker's Guide to the Galaxy, in which he played Arthur Dent, the last man to survive the destruction of the Earth by aliens.

As well as leading roles in such comedy films as *The Good Night, The All Together, Nativity!* and *Swinging with the Finkels,* Martin has portrayed the artist Rembrandt for Peter Greenaway's *Nightwatching* and is one of the voice-talents in the Aardman Animations stop-motion film, *The Pirates!*

It was while working on the first series of *Sherlock,* which he was filming with fellow *Hobbit* star, Benedict Cumberbatch, that Martin heard about the casting call for *The Lord of the Rings* prequel. 'I did an audition tape but I didn't think much about it because I knew that just about everyone in the British Isles was up for the film along with half of America! However, as time went by and I found that I was in the frame for the part of Bilbo – and stayed there – I began to think that it would be a really good gig.'

Martin learned that the film's then director, Guillermo del Toro, was keen on him for the role,

'I'M IN *the ******* Hobbit*!' HE ANNOUNCED EXCITEDLY, 'AND, I *am* THE ******* HOBBIT!'

but when the reins passed to Peter Jackson, he wondered what the outcome would be for him. 'I did think that might be the end of my chances, but I got a fairly swift message saying that although the captain had changed, the ship was still sailing in the same direction. Then I met up with Peter, Fran and Philippa in the summer of 2010 and they were very open about wanting me to do it.'

But there were still issues that the actor felt had to be considered. 'I know it sounds like a no-brainer: "Do you want to play Bilbo in *The Hobbit*?" but there were things I had to think through. Not like whether a bigger film might be coming along, because clearly there *wasn't* a bigger film coming along! But personal issues to do with my life and my family, because to play the part would be a huge commitment.'

Martin found that his concerns were met with understanding. 'There was absolutely no sense that as multi Oscar-winners they were offering me this role for which I should be down on my knees in gratitude; they were completely respect-ful of the fact that I was thinking as a husband and a dad, which made me like them even more.'

Having decided to take the part, Martin finally read *The Hobbit*. 'I'm not a student of fan-tasy literature by any means but what I felt was that it was a book which you were able to read without having to be steeped in that particular tradition. I found it very English and very funny.'

Working with Peter Jackson has been an enjoy-able experience. 'How to describe Peter's style? Well, it's fun, informal, direct and very unpreten-tious. I didn't get it straight away – though I'm not sure he got me straight away either! – but after a couple of weeks, a kind of shorthand grew up between us. Basically, I like to do every take slightly differently, partly because I get bored if I do the same thing over and over again, but also to be able to present Peter with options when he comes to edit the film. If a director says to you: "That was great can you do the same again?" it makes you think, "Why? Why not try something different?" So, I love providing choices and, fortunately, Pete

ABOVE: *Martin and Peter both dressed to impress in Hobbiton, while 1st AD Carolynne Cunningham looks on.* RIGHT: *Bilbo and the Dwarves in a tight spot.*

is open to all kinds of ideas.'

At an early press conference, Martin made headlines by his use of an expletive that would not be part of Mr Baggins' daily vocabulary. 'I'm in *The ******* Hobbit*!' he announced excitedly, 'And, I *AM* the ****** hobbit!'

Well, he may be playing the title character, but for much of the time he shares the screen with thirteen Dwarves.

'I wasn't daunted by that,' he says, 'because acting with other people is always more fun than acting on your own. The more the merrier! We are like a village community, which is all to the good because there have been some trying times during the filming and there will be others ahead – the more people you share that with the easier it becomes.'

Coming to terms with some of the techni-cal complications of filming *The Hobbit* were

a little testing to begin with. 'You find yourself doing things that feel like lunacy until you realize that they really work. I played a scene with Hugo Weaving as Elrond where I was on my knees, which felt kind of weird until I thought: it's just like playtime! The kind of thing three-year-olds do without thinking about it: stand on a chair and you're tall, go down on your knees and you're small! I love the fact that one minute we are working with the highest high-end technology available to anyone outside of NASA and the next we are playing like children. Peter will use whatever works. The only thing that is set in stone is that the film has to be king.'

The Hobbit is the story of a journey and, for Martin, filming these movies is also rather like a journey: 'You're embarking on the unknown, committing two years of your life to a project without knowing how things will unfold and develop. And because this feels like a journey, if you were to ask me to describe Bilbo's character I really couldn't do it – at least not while the journey is going on. What I do know is that his character undergoes a dramatic alteration. He is completely changed by the end of the book, as if the world he lives in, Middle-earth, has slapped him round the face and woken him up.'

Returning to the theme of change that runs through the book and the films, Martin says: 'If you'd ask me how Bilbo's character changes, I'd say through experience. He doesn't suddenly become brave; it is only experience that tells him he is able to stand his ground and does not have to be quite so scared. Bilbo comes back from his adventure as a 3D person where he may have been a bit 2D before!'

The actor is also well aware that playing Bilbo may impact on his own life. 'It would be disingenuous to say that it won't affect my future career, because – whether I'm good or bad in the films – more people will see them than anything else I've ever done or, possibly, ever will do in my life.'

He thinks a moment and then furrows that brow: 'It's a strange thing to think that long after I have stopped working or am even alive, people will see this film and will think of me as Bilbo Baggins; that's a strange gift to receive. In fact, I'm not even sure that it *is* a gift, maybe the real gift is just in doing work that you enjoy and doing that work as well as you can.'

Clothes Lines

ANN MASKREY ON DRESSING BILBO

'As the main character, Bilbo needs to be spot-on. My first question was: "Do we need to stay with the red waistcoat and grey dogtooth jacket worn by Ian Holm as Bilbo in the flashback scene in *The Fellowship of the Ring* where he picks up the ring?"

'When the decision was taken to give Bilbo a new look for *The Hobbit*, we put a variety of colour combinations on models in the workshop for Peter to look at. He took the jacket from one and put it with the waistcoat and trousers of another option and we began sourcing fabrics that would work well with the chosen colour palette. The result is a burgundy corduroy jacket, a green wool waistcoat with brass acorn-shaped buttons, caramel coloured needle-cord trousers and a stripey green and ochre neckerchief.

'Bilbo's other main outfit in the first film is what we call his 'good morning waistcoat', which he is wearing when he first encounters Gandalf outside Bag End. He also has a beautiful dressing gown that became a favourite with everybody, including Martin. Homely and cosy, it has echoes of Bilbo's smoking jacket in *Rings* and is made from pieces of silk brocade, velvet, cord and damask patchworked together. It is jewel-like while still looking as if his mum had made it from old curtains, cushions and bedspreads. Very distinctive and pleasing.'

OPPOSITE: *Bilbo wonders who might be outside his door.* ABOVE: *Ann Maskrey's costume designs showing Bilbo in his travelling outfit, nightshirt and fancy dressing gown.* INSET: *One of Bilbo's acorn buttons from his travelling waistcoat.*

Cutting Actors Down to Size

'Every Dwarf had to be seen differently. From the outset, Peter was adamant: the viewer had to be able to identify every Dwarf from a distance. This meant we had to create thirteen iconic figures, each with a unique look and a distinctive weapon.'

| DWALIN | BIFUR | BOFUR | NORI | DORI | ORI |

Richard Taylor is sitting in the kitchen at Weta Workshop in front of a display case containing creatures, props and miniature models dating back to his earliest collaborations with Peter Jackson on such films as *Meet the Feebles*, *Braindead* and *Heavenly Creatures*. Demands for work that is 'distinctive', 'unique' and 'iconic' are all part of daily life at Weta, and an ability to respond creatively to such requests is what has earned Richard his five Academy Awards for two films in *The Lord of the Rings* trilogy and *King Kong*.

'What made it challenging,' says Richard, 'is that we were just twelve weeks out from commencing shooting and, despite all the work we had done for *Rings*, we had done comparatively little on the development of Dwarf characters. Gimli was just one among thousands of characters. With *The Hobbit* we knew that we were seriously going to have to address the depiction of Dwarven culture.'

There was also a pressing practical question that needed resolving: 'We knew that Peter would cast the Dwarves on the actors' abilities, rather than for their stature, but having an actor who may be six-foot-three and knowing you've got to have him represent a character of four-foot-eight poses some interesting challenges.'

Stature is conveyed by the body-to-head ratio, which in the case of a Dwarf would be 5:1, whereas a six-foot actor has a body-to-head ratio of 8:1. The trick that had to be achieved was to make a normally proportioned human appear to have a larger head and shorter body.

From their extensive experience, Weta Workshop knew that to carry off this illusion they would have to utilize prosthetic make-up. However, Peter was anxious to avoid some of the problems that had been encountered with the make-up worn by John Rhys Davies as Gimli in

ABOVE: *Dwarves line up in their underthings.* OPPOSITE: *Adam Brown (Ori), wearing his ventilated foam skullcap.* RIGHT: *John Callen (Oin) stares out from his oversized head.*

Rings, which had proved both time-consuming to apply and uncomfortable to wear.

'Peter felt very strongly,' says Richard, 'that, as far as possible, the prosthetics had to stay above the eyes in order to speed up the daily application process and, by keeping the lower face free, allow the actors greater flexibility for facial performance.'

With that challenge in mind, the workshop began designing and created over six hundred initial conceptual drawings from which Peter could choose. Then, as soon as the actors were in place, casts were made of their heads and the selected design concepts for the Dwarves' faces and hair were sculpted in Plasticine over likenesses of the actor's features. These three-dimensional designs were eventually translated into individual items of moulded silicon make-up, transforming thirteen humans into thirteen Dwarves, giving each a distinct personality as well as a shared look that defined the Dwarvish temperament. 'We're an ornery bunch,' says Peter Hambleton, playing Gloin, 'but we pack a real punch. We are round, solid and chunky and that image is enhanced by our clothes, boots and even our hair.'

The size of the actors' heads appears to be widened by the use of a foam skullcap (helpfully punctuated with ventilation holes) over which are fitted the facial features, including heavier foreheads and eyebrows and more protuberant noses. Nori's Jed Brophy explains: 'Dwarves are an entirely different

race: they were fashioned out of the earth and they've got a very earthy feel to them.'

They also have large ears set lower on the head, a feature that, as John Callen playing Oin reveals, can be the cause of occasional minor difficulties: 'Now and again, the holes in my Dwarf ears don't quite match up with the holes in my own and I spend an entire day in something of a haze, not quite hearing what anybody says. However, since Oin is supposed to be deaf it's not been too much of a problem!'

Once the prosthetics have been applied, the make-up artists give each character a personal skin tone with unique detailing – including scars, skin blemishes and liver spots — all of which makes it impossible to tell where flesh ends and silicon begins.

The level of facial coverage varies from character to character. The younger Dwarves like Fili, Kili and Ori have little more than slightly larger noses requiring around thirty minutes to apply, while the older members of the Company with much heavier features can spend up to two-and-a-half hours each morning in the make-up chair. By far the most demanding prosthetic, both for the actor and for the person applying it, is that worn by Stephen Hunter as Bombur who, after a three-hour visit to the hair and make-up rooms, has his face entombed within a vast mass of silicon jowls and double chins.

The process is one that, even after months of wearing make-up, actors still find intriguing. Richard Armitage, playing Thorin, says: 'There is nothing quite like looking at yourself in the mirror and seeing somebody totally different looking back at you. It's like a dream. And there's no better way for an actor to "get into character", because fifty per cent of the work is already done for you!'

James Nesbitt is particularly attached to his nose: 'The great love of my life once told me that I didn't really have a nose, which is true. In real life I've nothing more than a snoot; but as Bofur I've got quite a large nose, which is nice. In fact, when we're finished, I'm going to take it home with me.'

Having designed the Dwarf prosthetics, Weta Workshop then had to cope with the further logistical problems resulting from the need for multiple sets of prosthetics to be worn by the various stand-in scale or stunt doubles. 'I don't know if this is an unprecedented undertaking,' says Richard Taylor, 'but having thirteen lead characters in prosthetics of this quality with so many duplications and variations in scale has required us to produce no less than forty individual facial silicon appliances… every day of filming.'

Wigs created by Hair and Make-up Designer, Peter King, further enhance the illusion that the Dwarf actors' heads are larger, while their beards hide the all-too obviously human neck, further helping the characters appear shorter and stockier. Full foam body suits worn under the costumes complete those iconic shapes ranging from lean and mean, via muscular to hugely overweight.

ABOVE: *Peter celebrates building his Dwarf barbecue.* OPPOSITE: *The Dwarf actors were cooled down between takes with ice-water pumped into vests under their costumes.*

With their body suits and costumes, the actors are carrying 30 kilos or more in addition to their own body weight and that – especially in scenes involving a lot of action – makes it a serious challenge keeping cool.

One solution is to wear a cooling vest similar to those used by racing drivers. Worn under the costume, they can be plugged in between takes and pumped through with ice-cold water to lower the body temperature.

Also, while waiting to film, the actors can use specially constructed cooling tents with large-scale chairs to accommodate their sized-up bodies. 'On the second day of filming,' recalls Aidan Turner who plays Kili, 'we were all complaining about how hot we were and how we needed somewhere, like a big tent, with loads of air conditioning pumping in where we could all hang out and wait in the cool. The next day, it was done! So now, if you've done a big scene and you're sweating, you can get into the chiller and it works wonders.' He then adds, confidentially: 'Actually, it can be a bit *too* cold! We all stoically chill for a while but, because we complained about being too hot, nobody now wants to complain about being too cold!'

The Dwarf cast also consumes considerable quantities of electrolyte drinks that aid re-hydration without increasing the need to use the toilet – a procedure that, for anyone in a Dwarf costume, has its own intimate difficulties…

Despite the precautions, sweating is a major hazard for Dwarves under the hot studio lights. 'If you do a scene and work up a little sweat,' says Aidan, 'you immediately feel it start to flow, which leads to the need for Dwarven irrigation.' Richard Armitage describes this less-than-pleasant process: 'Perspiration runs down, combines with the pros-

'I CAN'T GRUMBLE,' HE SAYS, 'BECAUSE IT'S THE BEST JOB IN THE WORLD, BUT THERE ARE TIMES WHEN I HAVE TO SMILE WHEN I HEAR SOME OF THE OTHER GUYS GOING ON AND ON ABOUT THEIR NOSE BEING A LITTLE BIT ITCHY!'

thetic glue and collects in little pools underneath our silicon eyebrows. Prosthetics Supervisor, Tami Lane, squeezes these little reservoirs and projectile sweat shoots out of your head. We refer to it as being "milked"!'

For William Kircher, who plays Bifur, the problem area is not his eyebrows: '*My* sweat comes out through my nose, which is highly embarrassing. All I can do is ask for a tissue and a cotton bud

and stick it up my nose. Incidentally, the one thing you don't want if you're wearing prosthetics is a cold. I've had one: it's a nightmare and there's absolutely nothing you can do.'

Additional Dwarven accessories include, for Dwalin, a pair of mighty silicon forearms, while most of the others wear silicon gloves to create stumpy fingered Dwarf hands. Once again, however, it is Stephen Hunter who carries the heaviest burden. 'I can't grumble,' he says, 'because it's the best job in the world, but there are times when I have to smile when I hear some of the other guys going on and on about their nose being a little bit itchy!'

Certainly Stephen has the sympathy of Adam Brown, playing Ori with minimal make-up and a relatively small body suit: 'Every time I'm tempted to complain about being hot, I just have to look at Stephen and I think: "Okay, but I'm not really *that* hot, am I?"'

Finally, a helpful hint from William Kircher for any Dwarf actor who develops one of those annoying itches: 'Since you can't scratch it, you just have to tap the itch, and *keep on* tapping it until the itching stops!'

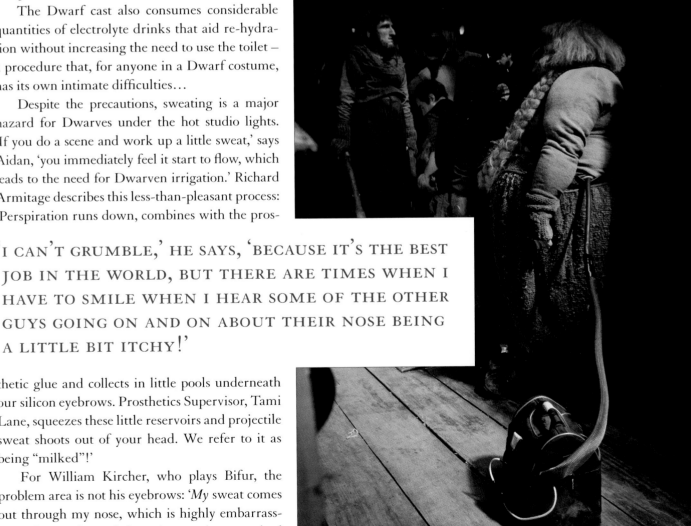

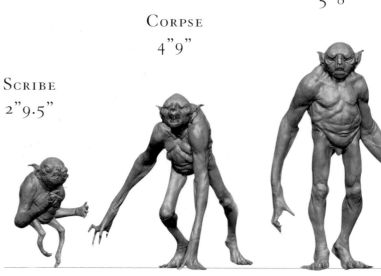

SCRIBE
2"9.5"

CORPSE
4"9"

NEW
GRINNAH
5"8"

TOP: *A wizard team: Peter stands between two Gandalfs: 'Tall'*
Paul Randall and Ian McKellen. ABOVE: *Seeing double:*
Stephen Hunter stands behind his small-scale double. RIGHT:
Scale height charts were crucial reference tools for every
department.

Matters of Scale

As well as devising ways for making thirteen human-sized actors appear to have the stature of Middle-earth Dwarves, the filmmakers had to grapple with how to manage their appearance in scenes where they are required to interact with larger characters such as Gandalf, the Elves of Rivendell and the mis-shapen Goblins. To create the illusion of such differences in scale, Peter Jackson and his associates drew on the vast experience gained in filming *The Lord of the Rings*. The demands of the more sophisticated High Definition and 3D technology employed on *The Hobbit* ruled out the use of some of the more basic tricks of the trade, such as 'forced perspective', that had previously enabled Frodo to ride alongside Gandalf on the wizard's cart or the hobbits and Gimli to participate at the Council of Elrond.

As in the earlier films, however, many of the characters in *The Hobbit* have large- or small-scale doubles that can stand in for them when different races have to share the screen. For example, a scene where Thorin is talking to Gandalf is likely to involve close-up shots of Richard Armitage and Ian McKellen, as well as long shots of Richard seen with Ian's large-scale double, Paul Randall, or from another angle Ian with Richard's small-scale double, Mark Atkins.

More complex shots – such as Gandalf and the Dwarves' meeting with Bilbo in Bag End – were created using motion-control cameras that film the actors on differently scaled sets. Ian McKellen's Gandalf, isolated in a small-scale version of the Baggins hobbit hole (making him appear big enough to bang his head on the doorways) could be shown talking with and reacting to the Dwarves on the Bilbo-scale Bag End set. While such scenes are hugely effective in portraying a world in which disparity of size is just part of normal daily life, achieving them is complex and demanding work, requiring everyone involved to move and deliver dialogue with choreographed precision.

As every successful conjuror knows, the best magic show uses a variety of different tricks and cheats, so that at any moment it's difficult – if not impossible – to say how the hand has deceived the eye. Similarly, the special effects in *The Hobbit* combine any number of techniques to create convincingly realistic cinematic illusions.

GOBLIN KING
10"

THORIN
5"

BILBO
4"11.5"

GANDALF
5"11"

ABOVE: *An actor prepares: Richard Armitage becomes Thorin.* RIGHT: *The Dwarf who would be King.*

Thorin

'**P**eter Jackson doesn't know this,' confides Richard Armitage, 'but I'm using a bit of him in the way I play the character of Thorin. Peter shows and commands great loyalty. That quality – to inspire and be inspired by loyalty – forms an important aspect of my portrayal of Thorin, and it comes directly from Peter.'

Standing at six feet two inches, Richard recalls being offered the role: 'After laughing at the idea, I started wondering, "How do I play somebody short?" Then immediately I thought, "Well, I need to do the opposite: I need to play somebody who *believes* they're tall, who believes they belong to a tower-

ing race." The Dwarves have huge underground kingdoms, so as far as they're concerned, they *are* six-foot-two.'

Richard is steeped in both the Tolkien and Jackson versions of life in Middle-earth: 'I read *The Hobbit* when I was growing up – it was one of those books that really got me excited about literature and made me want to become an actor. In fact, one of the first times I was ever on stage I played an Elf in a version of *The Hobbit*. I was also a mad fan of *The Lord of the Rings* trilogy and watched the films over and over. I secretly wish I had been in them – in fact, not so secretly! The first time I was on set looking into the eyes of Ian McKellen, I was desperately trying to stay in character while something inside me kept saying, "*That's Gandalf!*"'

Richard's early acting work included a part in the television film, *Cleopatra*, and appearances in the series *Cold Feet* and *Between the Sheets* while, in the cinema, he was seen in small roles in *This Year's Love* and *Star Wars Episode 1: The Phantom Menace,* and most recently in *Captain America: The First Avenger.* He came to public notice playing nineteenth-century mill-owner, John Thornton, in the TV serialization of Elizabeth Gaskell's *North and South,* followed by 37 episodes as Sir Guy of Gisborne in the popular adventure series, *Robin Hood,* and three seasons of the cult espionage drama, *Spooks* (televised in the USA as *MI-5*), in which he portrayed the enigmatic Lucas North.

On the day of his audition for *The Hobbit*, Richard was suffering with an injury sustained filming a stunt on *Spooks*: 'I had taken so many painkillers that I hobbled into the room, sat on my hands and the whole meeting passed in a bit of a blur. If nothing else, I think, with my audition I may have succeeded in showing my ability to convey pain!'

The character of Thorin Oakenshield, autocratic leader of the Company of Dwarves, is one that, for Richard, has a Shakespearian stature: 'I look at the character of Thorin and see echoes of Macbeth: the megalomania, the obstinacy, the tragedy of snowballing towards an inevitable fate he knows he cannot escape because it is the path he has to tread. The role has epic classicism to it and you have to be brave and play that.'

Richard is very aware that he is playing the role considerably younger than the depiction in the book. 'Thorin shouldn't be played as an old man, but as a mighty warrior who, rekindled and reignited, comes back into his prime to lead the Dwarves' quest to recover their treasure. You need to believe that he has enough fire in him to be King again. Thorin needs to be physically capable of achieving that and showing there is still a future for the Dwarves. In my portrayal, his age is more about his experience and his authoritarian personality than his actual years.'

A particular concern for Richard was Tolkien's description of Thorin having a beard that is considerably longer than the one he has grown for the film. 'I needed to find a reason for this and when I read Thorin's account of how when his grandfather and father, Thrór and Thráin, came out of the Lonely Mountain after the attack by Smaug the dragon, they had singed beards. This gave me the solution: he has cut his beard short, as a mark of respect to the

indignity suffered by them. Perhaps if he ever gets to sits on his throne again as king he'll grow a big old beard and tuck it into his belt, just like Tolkien wanted!'

Tolkien's Dwarves fascinate Richard: 'You could make an entire film just about the history of the Dwarves. In *The Lord of the Rings* Tolkien really only concentrates on one Dwarf, Gimli, but in *The Hobbit* he is interested in the character of the Dwarves as a race.'

This fascination underpins Richard's performance in the film: 'If you have knowledge of a character, you'll naturally communicate it, because you can sense history in people. They don't necessarily have to tell you about it, sometimes it is simply written on their faces. As an actor, if you know the history of other characters then – even if the camera never sees it – you find you're not looking at another actor in a costume on a film set, but instead are looking at a real person. I love it! Piecing it all together and firing up my imagination so I can really live as the character.'

'I know there are a million people out there for whom I will probably not be their version of Thorin, but I can only be *my* version of Thorin. Yet even that is elusive, and I still don't know whether I can achieve what I want to do with the role. Peter thinks I can do it, thinks I can get there; so I trust his judgement and hopefully we'll get there together. And that's exciting because an experience like this doesn't come along very often.'

ABOVE: *Richard was thrilled to act opposite 'Gandalf' himself, Ian McKellen.* OPPOSITE: *In full Thorin costume. The Dwarves need their colour-coded hoods in the Misty Mountains.*

Clothes Lines

ANN MASKREY ON DRESSING THORIN & CO

'Tolkien describes the colour of the hoods that the Dwarves hang up in Bag End but that made me think of garden gnomes, which is really not an image you want to give the movie audience! The one thing you don't want in a film is something that draws the eye to it and takes away from the creation as a whole.

'However, as a nod to one of the only bits of costume description Tolkien provides, the inside of the Dwarves' cape hoods feature the key colours mentioned by the author.

'Apart from the hoods, the Dwarf costumes are 'colour-coded' as follows: Thorin, midnight blue; Balin, predominately red; Dwalin, khaki green; Bifur, rust; Bofur, a dirty, yellowy mustard; Bombur, tones of olive green; Fili, a slightly-mauve grey; Kili, teal blue; Gloin, blood red; Oin, brown; Nori, grey; Dori, mulberry colours; and Ori, soft lilac-grey.

'The fabrics used for the Dwarves are a mix of wool, silk, corduroy and moleskin with a lot of leather and suede decorated with angular detailing to give a Dwarven look – we even managed to create Dwarf designs on knitted scarves and waistcoats.'

'Does it like games, does it like to play?'

It is the turning point in Tolkien's telling of *The Hobbit*: separated from the Dwarves and lost in the Goblin tunnels under the Misty Mountains, Bilbo Baggins finds himself on the shore of an underground lake. This is the lair of Gollum, whom the author described as being 'as dark and darkness, except for two big round pale eyes in his thin face'.

Gollum challenges Bilbo to a riddle-guessing contest, agreeing to show him the way out of the mountain if the hobbit wins. Bilbo's riddle contest with Gollum and his discovery that he has accidentally found Gollum's 'precious' – a magic ring that has the power to make the wearer invisible – not only influences the rest of the adventure, it leads, sixty years later, to the events described in *The Lord of the Rings*.

The first readers of *The Hobbit* in 1937 didn't know the true significance of Bilbo having acquired the Ring,

but everyone who has watched the film trilogy knows that Gollum's 'birthday present' was, in fact, the One Ring, forged by Sauron in the fires of Mount Doom to give him mastery over the races of Elves, Dwarves and Men.

This key scene is the one Peter Jackson chose to begin his filming of *The Hobbit*. 'I decided,' he says, 'that we would just jump right into the Misty Mountain cave and an intense shooting session with Martin as Bilbo and Andy Serkis as Gollum.'

OPPOSITE: *Andy and Martin Freeman discuss the location of a certain gold Ring.* ABOVE: *Andy in full motion-capture suit and face-camera prepares to channel his inner Gollum.*

'We shot it over two weeks as a theatre piece,' recalls Andy, 'and we filmed the whole encounter consecutively as a single sequence, doing it over and over again, but in lots of different ways. This enabled Pete to work with just two actors and create something that was essentially about the characters as well as establishing a relationship and rapport with the rest of the filmmaking crew.'

It was Martin Freeman's first session on *The Hobbit* set and allowed him to find and establish the character of Bilbo: 'Filming the scene with Gollum was definitely the key to coming to understand the character of Bilbo Baggins. You could argue that it might have been easier if we had started with some scenes of him at Bag End, having his breakfast and being interrupted by the Dwarves, but by having to play him confronting Gollum gave me the opportunity to explore what he was like when he was in extreme peril.'

As well as having the dramatic tension of danger, the scene is rich in character comedy: 'Humour,' says Andy, 'is one of the things that marks out *The Hobbit* as being distinct from *The Lord of the Rings* and I hope that the humour of the riddle sequence will be something that comes through from Martin and I playing opposite one another.'

Philippa Boyens recalls watching the scene being filmed: 'It was very powerful to realize that here were two excellent actors who clicked immediately and were pushing each other and playing off each other in exactly the right way.'

'Andy was alarmingly good,' says Martin, 'which meant that I had to be good. Fortunately, Bilbo and I had one thing in common: he had to be able to stand up to this extraordinary character, Gollum, and I had to be able to hold my own against this amazing actor who plays him!'

For Andy Serkis it was an opportunity to play out a scene that is briefly glimpsed as a flashback in *The Fellowship of the Ring*: 'It was just a tiny moment from the scene which we have filmed for *The Hobbit* but there's a sense of homage in the new film, which audiences will pick up on and be familiar with. Of course, when we filmed the flashback scene for *Rings* we had no idea that we would ever be recreating it in full!'

Living on an island in the lake, Gollum has a boat: a coracle similar to the one he used when he was still a hobbit-like creature named Sméagol, as depicted by Andy in the opening scenes of *The Two Towers*. On this occasion, however, Gollum's boat is made out of skin and bones, though it is probably best not to enquire who or what provided the boat-building materials!

For Andy it was an opportunity to play Gollum as a little less destroyed by his lust for the Ring than he is on the journey to Mordor with Frodo and Sam. So, how would he describe his character in the Riddle scene? He laughs: 'Well, he's sixty years younger and looking much better for it! He hasn't got as many scars on his back, because he hasn't been tortured, and he's got more teeth. He is hot, you know!'

Martin Freeman was acutely aware of the fact that Andy Serkis *was* Gollum: 'It's not very often, as an actor, that you get to film a scene with another character who is already so clearly established in popular culture. As soon as I started acting with Andy and he started speaking in that voice, I thought to myself: it's really him! This *is* Gollum!'

It is something that the film's director also acknowledges: 'Andy knows the character so well,' says Peter. 'The other day we were shooting a sequence where Bilbo had to do something with the Ring; I was talking with Andy and I said: "The thing you have to remember is that when you're holding this ring…" and then I suddenly stopped and thought, "How stupid! I'm talking to Gollum about the Ring! He knows exactly what this Ring does!"'

> 'IT WAS VERY POWERFUL TO REALIZE THAT HERE WERE TWO EXCELLENT ACTORS WHO CLICKED IMMEDIATELY AND WERE PUSHING EACH OTHER AND PLAYING OFF EACH OTHER IN EXACTLY THE RIGHT WAY.'

Return Tickets to Middle-earth

'All those actors who have come back are having a blast!' says Peter Jackson. 'We never had any trouble in their coming back because they didn't think they'd ever get to play those roles again!'

Returning cast members from *The Lord of the Rings* trilogy are Cate Blanchett as Galadriel, Orlando Bloom as Legolas, Andy Serkis as Gollum, Hugo Weaving as Elrond, Elijah Wood as Frodo and a trio of knights: Sir Christopher Lee as Saruman, Sir Ian Holm as old Bilbo and Sir Ian McKellen as Gandalf the Grey.

'People want to know, "Were you keen to come back to play Gandalf?"' says Ian. 'Yes, of course! Was I *really excited*? Less than you might think. It was a part I'd played. Was it going to be the same without all my friends from *The Lord of the Rings*? Who were all these Dwarves? But even though it was clearly going to be a very different project, an awful lot of elements remained the same, so once details about the project became clear I was very happy. Of course, anyone could have played the part, really. It's all too easy: you just stick on a beard, do a rough voice, and there you are! Mind you, in my heart of hearts, I would have not been happy if some other actor had been playing Gandalf.'

Ian was particularly concerned how Tolkien's book would be adapted for the screenplay: 'Gandalf in *The Hobbit* is pretty central to the story, but he's not there all the time: he sets up the journey that the Dwarves and the hobbit go on, and then he's off somewhere else, doing other business, and quite what that is is not revealed in the novel. Peter's promised that, in the films, we would get to see what Gandalf was up to when he wasn't on the journey. That decision allowed the screenwriters to put the adventure in *The Hobbit* into the context of what was happening in Middle-earth, which is important because the Dwarves' journey is rather a selfish one. Unlike the Fellowship in *Rings*, the Dwarves are not out to save Middle-earth; they're just out to regain their old strength and power, land and riches. As the story is now being told, you see how the world explored by Bilbo becomes the universe experienced by Frodo. It's true to the once-upon-a-time nature of *The Hobbit* and the more epic story of *The Lord of the Rings*.'

Ian experienced an emotional moment when getting a preview of a compilation of early footage. 'Suddenly up on the screen came Ian Holm, looking like he always did as old Bilbo. And I was just recovering from the delightful shock of seeing him again in that character when the door of Bag End opened and in walked Elijah Wood and the tears welled up. It wasn't nostalgia; it was just thrilling that they both still wanted to be involved. But of course they did!'

Elijah confirms that view: 'I was overjoyed to come back: it was an opportunity to revisit a time in my life that had passed and have another peek into the world I'd left behind. It felt like a chance for a massive family reunion. With a number of original cast members returning, and so many of the crew and creative heads taking up their old jobs again, it feels like stepping back in time.'

So what does Elijah feel about becoming Frodo once again? 'It's a beautiful thing to be able to reprise the role without the enormity of the burden; to come back – almost like a vacation – and say hello to an old friend. For audiences, I think having so many of the original cast involved immediately gives you a wash of familiarity amongst the things that are unfamiliar.'

Despite the cameo nature of the role, Elijah experienced some extraordinary moments: 'I got chills reading the script, when Frodo hears that Gandalf is on his way and he runs off, telling Bilbo that he's going to the Eastfarthing woods to await Gandalf's arrival. As everyone who's seen *The Lord of the Rings* knows, you see Frodo for the first time sitting reading in a tree and listening for the sound of Gandalf's cart to come along the road. Now, here we were filming the moment immediately before that happens.'

But he is also conscious that there have been one or two developments on set and off: 'Bag End,' says Elijah, 'is bigger than I remember it – Bilbo certainly seems to have been busy with the home improvements! The other significant advance is *these*!'

OPPOSITE: *The unique and irreplaceable Ian McKellen returns as Gandalf.* LEFT: *Elrond and Gandalf, together again.* ABOVE: *Peter and Elijah: 'You haven't changed a bit!'*

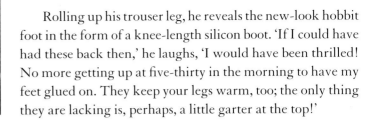

Rolling up his trouser leg, he reveals the new-look hobbit foot in the form of a knee-length silicon boot. 'If I could have had these back then,' he laughs, 'I would have been thrilled! No more getting up at five-thirty in the morning to have my feet glued on. They keep your legs warm, too; the only thing they are lacking is, perhaps, a little garter at the top!'

'EVEN THOUGH WE'VE ALL CHANGED TO SOME EXTENT, THERE'S A LANGUAGE THAT WAS ESTABLISHED ON THE PREVIOUS FILMS THAT YOU CAN EASILY SLIP BACK INTO.'

For Hugo Weaving, playing Elrond, there was a significant difference to his experience of playing the role in *The Lord of the Rings*: 'It's been slightly strange this time around because I didn't have a script until I got here. But that's part of the nature of working with Pete: his particular process is one where, in a way, you have to surrender yourself completely to what he's into on the day. And it's a great process; I have to prepare as much as I can and then just let everything go and be as open as possible to work with him. He has a fantastic ability to be buoyant and creative and kind of cheeky. It is fun because Pete's got a great spirit that I really enjoy.'

There was also, as Hugo discovered, much else that was, happily, very familiar: 'The similarities are to do with personalities: coming back and meeting the same people throughout the cast and crew who were involved with *Rings*. Even though we've all changed to some extent, that's really lovely and grounding and there's a language that was established on the previous films that you can easily slip back into.'

Ian McKellen agrees: 'I am working with so many of the same people I worked with on *The Lord of the Rings* – not just the director, screenwriters and cinematographer, but also my dresser and make-up artist. So, it's very much like coming home; but it's not about nostalgically thinking, "Ah, it's just like being back in the old days!" No, it's not the *old* days; it's the *same* days, really.'

LEFT: *Cate Blanchett deep in thought in Rivendell.*
ABOVE: *Hugo Weaving has his 'Elven ventilation' fitted!*

IAN McKELLEN

Wizard Notions on Being Gandalf

'I'm not sure whether people realize that I wear a false nose.' Ian McKellen is talking about being Gandalf. 'A lot of characters in these films wear false noses. I don't know what it is. It just seems to help. But I think my nose is even bigger than it was the first time I was Gandalf, and it's changed subtly. Maybe my own face has changed, and the new nose is keeping up with it. But I suspect if people don't know that, they'll think, "Ah, there's the Gandalf I remember!"'

OPPOSITE: *Gandalf the Grey returns to Bag End.* ABOVE: *Ian discusses his next scene with Peter Jackson while standing in Trollshaw Forest.*

The fact that our memories of Gandalf are inextricably linked with *The Lord of the Rings* and the journey of Frodo Baggins prompts Ian to reflect on how Frodo's character contrasts with that of his uncle, Bilbo, whose story is told in *The Hobbit*.

'Bilbo is not Frodo. Frodo is the little lad who goes off to save the world. Bilbo is more settled in his ways. He's absolutely adamant that he doesn't want to go on any journey – "Oh, no. I don't want adventures. I'm not that sort of person at all!" There's a dullness to him that Gandalf doesn't like and wants to shake out of him. So, Bilbo's journey is one of self-revelation: learning about himself and discovering a world that he could never have anticipated. And, having been on that journey, he's changed for ever both by the events he witnesses and by what he brings back with him – namely, the Ring.'

The venture on which Thorin, the Dwarves and Bilbo embark is daring and dangerous, but it is all part of the wizard's plan: 'Gandalf has been around for a very long time. He knows everybody. And he's a rather hands-on person: he's not sitting in an office sending messages to the world, he's out there, walking and riding about the place, holding meetings, having talks. Gandalf organizes, puts people together, makes things happen. The reason he helps Thorin is not just because he sympathizes with the Dwarves' desire to regain their lost empire and wealth, but because it might be good for Middle-earth. There is, after all, the ever-present danger of the dragon: will it reawaken and cause more havoc? Can that threat be contained – and are the Dwarves the people to help do that? And, beyond that, there are other issues: Middle-earth is beginning to rumble and tumble; forces are at work; things are changing – and not for the better.'

As Ian explains, Gandalf's wisdom is rooted in centuries of knowledge and personal experience: 'He is so old – almost three thousand years – that he can put the current situation into the context of recent and past history, enabling him to make the judgement that now is the time to help the Dwarves.'

But why choose a hobbit to take part in this hazardous mission? 'Well,' laughs Ian, 'I think Gandalf is a bit of an optimist; he looks for the good in people whether they are Dwarves, Elves or hobbits, and he particularly likes the ways of hobbits. He enjoys their company. They amuse and charm him. You feel that if Gandalf were to have a home, he might like it to be on the outskirts of Hobbiton, where he could eat and drink and smoke and pass the time of day with these curious folk. And he sends Bilbo on this adventure – or, rather, *throws him into it!* – because he doesn't like the life that Bilbo is leading. Gandalf, aged, wise, much-travelled, is saying, "There's a world outside Hobbiton, and you'll be the better for having come into contact with it. So, come on Bilbo, join the real world!" Outsiders may say, "Oh, there goes Gandalf, meddling again, trusting the fate of this enterprise to an untried, untested hobbit." But Gandalf is a good judge of hobbits!'

After so many years of being associated with the character, would Ian McKellen – if such a thing were possible – like to meet and get to know Gandalf? 'Oh, yes, I think I'd like to know Gandalf! I feel about him in a way that, perhaps, it is inconceivable to feel about Galadriel or some of those other very impressive but austere characters. I mean, you can't imagine going for a good night out and having a knees-up with Galadriel, can you? Or Saruman. Or Elrond, really. But with Gandalf? Oh, yes, Gandalf would be there!'

Getting Fit for Filming

'As an actor, you'd be a fool not to have horse riding written down among the things you can do. I always lie about those things. At the audition, Peter asked, "What are you like with a sword and a horse?" I said: "Mate, brilliant! I can jump on cattle and gallop them anywhere! Just give me a whip and a sword. Slay everything!" I couldn't do *anything*! Never even held a sword in my life!'

ABOVE: *(From l-r) Jed Brophy, Aidan Turner and (far right) Mark Hadlow are taught how to fight like a Dwarf.* OPPOSITE: *Jed Brophy (Nori) and James Nesbitt (Bofur) enjoy life in the saddle.* OVERLEAF: *The Company of Thorin Oakenshield journeys east.*

Aidan Turner, who plays Kili, is talking about the 'boot camp' training that was daily life for the actors playing the thirteen Dwarves in the months leading up to the start of filming.

Looking back, John Callen, who plays Oin, says, 'The first time I met most of the other actors was at a social event, which was a useful way of meeting people because it was very relaxed. But I remember thinking: "We aren't being brought together to socialize. We are here to work, to produce a film." It was when we began working out in the gym, rehearsing movement, practising sword fighting and horse riding that real rapport started to develop among us as a group.'

It is a view shared by Jed Brophy, playing Nori: 'When you're having a one-on-one fight with another actor that you don't really know, you have to learn to trust that they're not going to hurt you and at boot camp we learnt to trust each other.'

There were other issues that had to be faced, as Peter Hambleton, playing Gloin, explains: 'Boot camp was intensive, action-packed and full-on and those of us who had maybe let ourselves go in recent years had to confront some challenges about our weight and fitness and had to work towards getting ourselves to a level where we could handle everything that we've got to do on this job. So it was tough, but in the most positive way.'

'Suddenly,' recalls Mark Hadlow, who plays Dori, 'I was doing stuff that I hadn't done in twenty years.' While Adam Brown, playing Mark's screen brother, Ori, confesses: 'Prior to this, I'd never done any exercise in my whole life!'

John Callen was aware of the need for mutual tolerance: 'I'm quite sure it was very frustrating for a number of other people who are so much more agile when we went through simple things like doing a forward roll. Who can't do a forward roll? *I* can't! Or at least, I *couldn't*. They taught me how to do that. We found that we all had strengths and weaknesses, but weaknesses were not a put down, because while one person might be better at one thing, another would be better at something else. For example, I had some skill as a horseman, whereas other people in the cast had never been on a horse.'

One virgin equestrian was Mark: 'My wife has trained thoroughbreds, ridden and jumped in shows. Both my daughters and my son ride. There was no one in my family who didn't ride a horse except me! The first time I'm on a horse, my wife is sitting there with her head in her hands, but now I love it! Boot camp was quite extraordinary and has given me a wonderful new lease on life.'

'When we first got together,' says William Kircher, who plays Bifur, 'we were just a bunch of individuals, but through those months of training together we have created an ensemble. The Dwarves in the film set out on a quest, a journey filled with danger and humour, good times and bad to recover their treasure from the Lonely Mountain. As a cast, we are on a parallel journey and our Mountain is the creation of these films.'

DEAN O'GORMAN

Fili

'Heart-throb Dwarves?' laughs Dean O'Gorman. 'That seems to be a contradiction in terms!' He is talking about the potential screen-appeal of his character, Fili, and that of his brother, Kili. 'The thing people don't know about Dwarves is that we start off handsome and get uglier as we get older! So they caught us two in our prime! As far as I'm concerned, I think the only following Fili is likely to have is among testosterone-filled guys who like to see people chopping up Goblins with two swords!'

Dean was cast to replace English actor, Rob Kazinsky, who left the production for personal reasons. 'I jumped onto a ship that was already sailing,' he says, adding, 'what's more, I thought the ship had long gone! I'd read about who was playing who in *The Hobbit* and knew that filming had started so, when I was asked to audition, I thought the best I could hope for might be a line or two as an Orc. I flew into Wellington on a Wednesday, auditioned with Aidan Turner and, the following Monday, was standing on his shoulders trying to hit a Troll in the face with an axe!'

A member of the Kiwi Dwarf contingent, Dean is well known to TV viewers in New Zealand as Anders Johnson (a reincarnation of the Norse god, Bragi) in the comedy drama series, *The Almighty Johnsons*, as well as for roles in *Serial Killers*, *McLeod's Daughters*, *Legends of the Seeker* and the long-running hospital drama, *Shortland Street*.

'My first day on set,' Dean recalls, 'I kept saying to myself, "This is nothing like *Shortland Street*!" It was surreal: I was walking around like a deer in the headlights. There were so many instant challenges: fitness training, voice and movement coaching, getting used to the costume, prosthetics and handling swords. But I think the biggest challenge was coming to grips with the vast scale of this production: the huge sets and the enormous numbers of people. On my very first day, it seemed like there were knights everywhere – Sir Peter Jackson, Sir Ian McKellen, Sir Richard Taylor – and I was just trying to remember what I was here to do and not get totally flummoxed by everything.'

Of his role as Fili, Dean says: 'He is the nephew of Thorin, who is very much a father figure to him and, while he is one of the younger, more exuberant Dwarves, he is respectful of

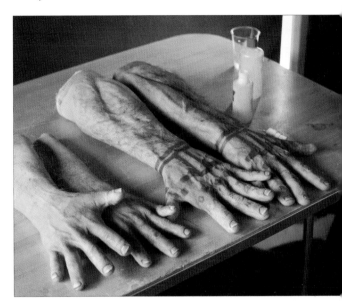

Thorin and very conscious that, in the event of anything happening to his uncle, he's next in line for the crown.'

The close relationship between Fili and Kili is crucial to understanding their characters and is informed by Dean's rapport with Aidan: 'The brothers are really close and do everything together: where one goes, the other goes, always running off ahead and doing stuff, looking round corners, checking things out. But although Fili can be a bit reckless at times, he is the more responsible of the two and feels protective of his younger brother. The great thing was that as soon

as Aidan and I met we clicked; we instantly knew we were going to get along and the more time we spend together, the more we've developed a brotherly bond that's helped us figure out the dynamic of our characters.'

As the first images of Fili and Kili were released it quickly became evident that these two were not typical Dwarves. 'I agree,' says Dean. 'Dwarves don't have the reputation for being cool, but I reckon Fili and Kili are going to bring back the coolness of Dwarves. Elves were last year! This year, the short guys are going to get a foot up and Dwarf chic is definitely going to be in!'

For Dean, one of the most pleasantly surprising aspects of playing Fili is the chance to fulfil an unusual ambition: 'I've always wished I had bigger hands and now I've got them! To help our Dwarven appearance – and to prevent us looking like chunky characters with tiny T-Rex hands – they made each of us a pair of good-sized silicon hands that fit like a glove. Filling a Dwarf pipe with tobacco can be tricky and handling a sword is a bit demanding, but they are amazing and I want to keep them and just wear them out one night, and order a beer!'

Looking back on the unexpected way in which he joined the *Unexpected Journey*, Dean reflects: 'I like jumping into things, and there's nothing like being booted into a project to motivate you to get out there and start doing it.'

Kili

'Essentially, I think of the fighting duo of Kili and Fili as the dream team!' This is how Aidan Turner, who plays one half of that team, describes the characters of himself and his screen brother. 'They see themselves as being at the forefront of the fighting constabulary. They are close to the royal family and they are eager to impress Thorin, but I don't think they're too well informed. They've grown up on the old songs and stories about the wars of the past and the various challenges that have confronted the Dwarves. But when they arrive at Bag End, this ensemble of misfits confronts them: they really don't know what they've let themselves in for.'

Irish-born Aidan Turner had played the poet and painter, Dante Gabriel Rossetti, in *Desperate Romantics*, a six-part television drama series about the nineteenth-century group of artists known as the Pre-Raphaelite Brotherhood, but it was perhaps another TV series that caught Peter Jackson's eye. *Being Human*, a hybrid of comedy and horror, featured the flat-sharing lives of a ghost, a werewolf and, Aidan's role, a vampire. 'Peter, being a lover of the macabre,' he recalls, 'was already aware of *Being Human*, which was a great help to me because I felt I didn't have to prove myself so much as I might have if he hadn't known anything about my work. I'm a typical actor in that I bounce about from one audition to the next, hoping that something will come of it and I'll manage to land a part. In this case, I was lucky and did!'

Reflecting on his role as Kili, Aidan says: 'At the outset, he is eager and a bit naïve, but a lot happens to him along the way. As Bilbo begins to come through and start saving the day, Kili – along with all the Dwarves – has to come to terms with the fact that brute force isn't necessarily the way in which they're going to win this fight. The journey is a massive and arduous learning curve for him, during which his ideas about everything begin to change.'

Playing one of the 'younger' Dwarves means that Aidan doesn't have to wear as much prosthetic make-up as some of the others. 'This is not my nose,' he says, giving it a tweak, 'but it's not much bigger than my own and it's roughly the same shape. I started out with heavier make-up across the whole of my forehead and down to my nose, but my features got reviewed and remodelled. I think it was particularly

BELOW: *Aidan, Dean & John Callen show off their new riding skills.* OPPOSITE: *One of the 'dream team': in the Hair & Make-up chair; the young Dwarf is armed and dangerous.*

important that the characters of Kili and Fili should seem quite youthful and the original prosthetics didn't help that look at all. Apart from which it makes my mornings in make-up a lot easier!'

Despite playing Dwarves, Aidan and fellow actor Dean O'Gorman are, predictably, being seen as potentially following in Orlando Bloom's Elvish footsteps as the new heart-throbs of Middle-earth: 'The Dwarves are a group of very distinct individuals who are attempting to operate as one, so it's very much an ensemble company, but since we are the youngest members of that company it is inevitable that our characters will be viewed in that way. When it comes to fan followings, who knows what will happen? All I can say is it sounds really exciting – but also quite terrifying!'

Dressing the Drama

'**W**orking on *The Hobbit* is full of variety: just when you think you don't want to see another Dwarven geometric pattern in your life, you suddenly find yourself in the Elven world and it's like working on a different movie!'

Over a cup of tea and a very English selection of biscuits – Garibaldis, custard creams and lemon puffs – Costume Designer, Ann Maskrey, is talking about the task of designing costumes for *The Hobbit* and the differences between working on a movie in New Zealand and in her homeland.

'If I was making a film like this in Britain,' she says, 'I would be diving into the costume houses and selecting various items off the racks in order to put together a certain look and would then create just one or two key pieces, whereas here everything is designed and made from scratch. And that means *everything*: even non-speaking characters who are three paces behind the central characters. It is, of course, a stack more work, but it is also a joy because I'm getting to do what – when I was eighteen and very naïve – I always thought a designer *would* do! What's more, I'm doing it on what is obviously the best project I could possibly have.'

Ann, who has worked on such films as *Batman Begins*, *The Fifth Element*, *The Duchess*, *Troy* and *Star Wars Episodes I, II* and *III*, explains that, however exciting the project, it always comes with a great many challenges. 'To start with,' she says, 'if we are buying materials from overseas – whether fabrics from India or a range of printed, pleated and embroidered leather from Italy – we have to allow enough time to have them shipped to New Zealand. Also, there are fewer resources here than you would find in London or Hollywood, in terms of fabric warehouses and specialist shops selling items such as buttons and buckles, but that makes you all the more creative and resourceful.'

How does the design process begin? 'The first thing to remember,' says Ann, 'is that there aren't any pattern books for designers of costume in Middle-earth! There's the precedent of what was done on *The Lord of the Rings* – the costumes for Gandalf and Saruman, for example, are the same as they were for the trilogy – and there's imagination. The design

process can begin with something very simple, such as a few squiggles in a notebook jotted down at two o'clock in the morning, that are later followed by more developed sketches. Pete chose the design for one costume from what was little more than a light pencil sketch, but even the roughest sketch has to give a clear idea of where the design is heading.'

Looking around the walls of her office, covered in sketches of Elves, hobbits and Dwarves, Ann says: 'You have to help the director tell the story he wants to tell and you hope that the costumes will help the actors find the characters they are playing. To my mind, designs are always the starting point for a costume, not necessarily the end product.'

Certainly a sketch, or even a finished design, can only ever give an impression of how it will look when it is made. Swatches of fabric are often attached to the designs but these are only scraps of material and it is not always easy to imagine how it would look as a finished coat or a dress.

'HERE EVERYTHING IS DESIGNED AND MADE FROM SCRATCH. AND THAT MEANS *everything*.'

'I absolutely adored the material I wanted to use for Galadriel's coat, but it was difficult to visualize from just one small piece how it would look when it was made. I know a lot about fabric and what they will do, and sometimes you simply have to make the whole garment and say, "Look what it does!" and then, hopefully, everyone say: "Yes, I get it now!"'

Sometimes a design idea gets knocked back. For Ann, that is simply an opportunity to re-think: 'One thing I've learned is that when an idea I liked isn't taken up by the filmmakers, I try to dig deep for something that is better. But I've also found that you shouldn't too readily dismiss your first ideas, because sometimes they come back from the dead!'

Walking round the costume workshop, we pass rack after rack, stacked with great bolts of cloth. One whole section is given over to the materials used for the Dwarves' costumes. 'This,' says Ann, 'is our equivalent of a police taped

incident area! No one can touch those bales for anything other than Dwarf costumes.'

One of the first decisions taken on the project, long before those costumes could be designed, was to settle what the Dwarves would look like *without clothes*. Ann explains: 'Peter wanted them to have physical individuality, so, once the actors were cast, we drew up a variety of body shapes. Peter then chose the look he wanted for each of the Dwarves from the athletic Fili and Kili to the chunky heavy-weight, Bombur.'

The next challenge was to find a way to give actors a body shape that was significantly different from their own. 'Years ago,' recalls Ann, 'I worked on *The Wind in the Willows* and we made a wire cage to change Terry Jones into the rotund Mr Toad. We initially tried a similar technique for the Dwarves with Peter Hambleton, who plays

Gloin, "test-driving" the apparatus. However, the actor felt that, rather than having a wire skeleton around his body, he needed to be able to feel his Dwarf body next to his own skin to have a sense of it being part of himself.'

The answer was body suits made in foam and covered in lycra, with the various jointed parts connected by elastic so as to simulate muscular movement, and designed so that the actor can unbutton and remove various sections, such as Bombur's substantial stomach, during breaks in filming.

Clothing the Dwarves became a huge undertaking because each of the thirteen characters has several sets of costume reflecting the wear and tear that the garments undergo on each stage of the journey. In addition, there are further costumes and body suits for the photo doubles, riding doubles, stunt doubles and scale doubles.

OPPOSITE: *Sylvester McCoy in full costume as Radagast the Brown.* ABOVE: *Four pretty young hobbit maids wearing sprigged cotton dresses with full skirts and petticoats embellished with embroidery and lace.*

THORIN BALIN DWALIN BIFUR BOFUR BOMBUR

FILI   KILI   GLOIN   OIN   NORI   DORI   ORI

'The issue of scale,' comments Ann, 'is quite problematic, because costumes worn by scale doubles have to be made from the same fabric as that worn by the main actor but, at the same time, have to be scaled up or down in order to match with the original. The same applies to buttons, belts and buckles; while anything done to make the costume look worn or damaged has to be replicated across the whole range of different costume worn by everyone playing or standing in for a character.'

The demands on the costume designer are great, but Ann sees only the rewards: 'I shall eventually be able to return home and ruffle the feathers of the six people or so who normally get asked to do the top designing jobs back in Britain. Also, I keep reminding myself that these films are going to be around for ever. The other week, my PA found a file of stuff in a Wellington charity shop relating to the costumes for *The Lord of the Rings* and bought it for a dollar. I reckon there will come a day when I'm doddering down the street to collect my pension and I'll see something in a charity shop about the films of *The Hobbit* and I'll say, "I did the costumes on that…" and no one will believe me because they'll think I'm just this batty old woman!'

TOP: *Costume designs of the Dwarves' individual shirts.* LEFT: *Bilbo and the Dwarves' costumes would require a multitude of different materials, even for a single character* (RIGHT).

BIFUR

Clothes Lines

Ann Maskrey on Dressing Galadriel

'At the White Council, Galadriel wears a coat in shot silk, woven with a metallic thread that magically catches the light. I originally drew the coat as if it were blowing in the wind, hoping that it would create an ethereal, enigmatic vision of Galadriel. While waiting for a decision on the design, we made up the coat and photographed it on a model and it looked beautiful.

'Unfortunately, when my drawing got looked at, it was interpreted as being a sketch for a big, sticky-out frock, which was absolutely not what was wanted!

'I moved on to designing alternative coat patterns, but none of them was working. During one discussion, Philippa Boyens suggested a particular style and I just sidled out the photograph of my original coat and innocently asked: 'What about this one?' And that became it!

'Beneath the coat, Galadriel wears a chiffon dress covered in rivulets of Swarovski crystals that look like running water over another shimmering layer of beaded chiffon. On the day of the shoot, the dress had dropped because of the weight of the rhinestones, so I had to cut a chunk off the front hem to avoid Cate Blanchett walking up inside her skirt and the disaster that would have followed!'

Sketchbooks in Wilderland

Take two very different artists, both with a formidable track record of interpreting the works of J.R.R. Tolkien, and put them in a room together in Wellington with paper, pencils and computer graphics tools and invite them to collaborate on the task of defining the look of the world seen in *The Hobbit*. The marriage of talents represented by the work of Alan Lee and John Howe has set the style for these films just as it did, ten years earlier, for *The Lord of the Rings*.

For creative individuals used to working on their own, it might have seemed an intimidating prospect. 'I would have found it impossible,' says John, 'to work with someone whose ideas I didn't respect and whose art I didn't admire, but to be working alongside Alan is very stimulating.'

Alan believes that their combined strength comes from their independent identities and separate, and unique, approach: 'We have very different perspectives. I feel John is very strong on the drama of the story and brings out more of the fantastical elements, whereas I am, probably, trying to focus more on what makes it real.'

'Collaborating with Alan,' says John, 'is hard in one respect only, in that there is this guy on the other side of the room who is constantly coming up with brilliant ideas! Again and again, I look at Alan's drawings and think, "I wish I'd had that idea!" But once that idea is there and is liked by Peter, there's an opportunity for both of us to elaborate on it.'

Alan agrees: 'I also see things in John's drawings that I'm eager to make part of mine and it is often the case that where one of us has the idea for the overall scheme for how a particular place will look, the other will be the one to focus on specific details within that scheme.'

And, as John adds: 'You have the comfort of knowing that whatever will appear, either you or your colleague will have provided most of those visuals. So when you see the results on the screen there is less to regret.'

One example of the combined talents of John and Alan is Radagast's house. 'We had designed him a home under a tree,' recalls John, 'and Peter's response was that this felt like an image that had been seen many times before and suggested that the tree might have grown up *through* the house. So, I did some drawings along those lines but they weren't quite working for Peter. Then Alan drew the gable of a house that had been split in two by a tree branch and I took that and added it to the top of the house I'd drawn, and that was virtually what was built.'

Many artists with lesser reputations than these two men might find it difficult to pour their creativity into a project where their artistry didn't receive the kind of recognition that goes with having their name on a book cover or exhibition catalogue. So how do John and Alan manage it?

'I deal with it,' says Alan, 'in the knowledge that it is not a permanent state. It is just for a limited period – albeit a *long* one! And that, in itself, is a consideration: during the time I was involved in *The Lord of the Rings* I could have produced four books that would now be providing me with an income. Although you don't really own the idea, it is someone else's commission and you don't get a royalty, the pluses outnumber the minuses. This is especially because you are involved in what is a huge collaboration that provides an opportunity to enjoy a much more social way of working than we usually experience.'

'Working at the Take-out Window, is how I refer to it,' responds John, 'because we do long hours and deliver a lot. But it's an opportunity that is not going to come again, and even though you are a very tiny cog in this huge machine that roars and grinds relentlessly along until the films come out, it's gratifying to know that you are a little cog somewhere near the beginning of the process, which sets the great wheel in motion.'

OPPOSITE: *Alan Lee and John Howe at ease on set.*

TOP TO BOTTOM: *Visions of Middle-earth: Bilbo and the Dwarves are taken to Goblin Town* (watercolour, John Howe); *Thorin's Company camps in Trollshaw Forest* (pencil, Alan Lee); *and a computer-generated sun in this montage of photos and painted elements heralds Gandalf's arrival and signals the end of the Trolls* (digital, Alan Lee).

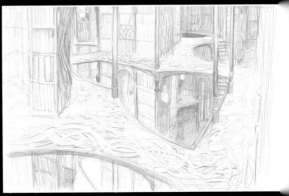

TOP TO BOTTOM: *Windows on Wilderland: Gandalf summons the fleeing Dwarves – the nearest bearing some resemblance to the artist – to potential safety* (watercolour, John Howe); *Bilbo enters Gollum's Cave, and a fateful meeting with its occupant* (watercolour, John Howe); *Elrond leads his Elf riders back to meet their unexpected guests* (pencil, Alan Lee); *the delicate Elven tracery in the walkway confirms the artist in Elven fevering part of the stunning library at Rivendell* (pencil, Alan Lee).

Casting Around

'**P**eople think there are thirteen Dwarves. But in fact there are *fifty-two* of them!' New Zealand Casting Directors, Liz Mullane and Miranda Rivers, are providing some surprising statistics about *The Hobbit*.

It transpires that every time you see a Dwarf on screen, you are looking at any one of four people. It could be the actor, or it might be his Second Unit double, stunt double or small-scale double.

On *The Lord of the Rings*, the biggest task faced by Casting was finding and wrangling vast hordes of extras; now, as Liz and Miranda explain, the major task on *The Hobbit* is locating enough large and small-scale doubles for the cast.

Nor is this just a Dwarf issue, because there are no less than seven Bilbos, including one small-scale double (long-serving hobbit-double from *Rings*, Kiran Shah) with a height of 4'1" and, depending on the requirements of perspective, a 4'11" 'mid-scale double'.

In the run-up to filming, the Casting team travelled through New Zealand's two islands, holding auditions for people who were over six feet ten inches or under five feet four. 'Some of the smaller people who came along,' recalls Liz, 'found that, for the very first time in their lives, they were too tall!'

However, as Miranda explains, there is more to casting than feet and inches: 'It's not simply about finding people who look right physically, it's about the need to find individuals who are going to be available when required – which means, if necessary, being prepared to uproot themselves and travel anywhere in the country at a moment's notice – and, most importantly, have a good personality that's not going to drive everyone else mad!'

'THANKS TO MODERN PHONES,' SAYS LIZ, 'PEOPLE CAN NOW PHOTOGRAPH THEIR HANDS, EARS AND NOSES AND SEND THEM IN FOR CONSIDERATION. THE DOUBLE BODY-PART BUSINESS HAS BEEN TOTALLY REVOLUTIONIZED BY MODERN TECHNOLOGY!'

The thirteen small-scale doubles, who are now a permanent part of the crew, were eventually selected from a shortlist of thirty hopefuls following a 'Scale Doubles Boot Camp'.

'We knew we had to take people with no previous experience,' says Liz, 'put them through a fitness regime, train them to do stunts – without killing themselves or anyone else – teach them how to act, and explain the etiquette and protocol of being on a movie set.'

The Dwarf scale doubles, who are men and women aged between nineteen and thirty, had to confront a number of challenges including, for the females, mimicking a male walk and, for both sexes, learning to look as if they had the 'heavy' qualities of the Dwarven race in contrast to their own natural light-footedness. They also had to come to terms with the physical demands of moving around in a heavy costume and wearing a mask replicating the features of the actor for whom they are doubling. The most exacting requirement,

however, is finding how to take on 'the essence' of that cast member so that, on film, it is impossible to spot the difference between actor and double.

Literally at the opposite end of the scale are the twenty-four tall people involved in the production. The casting department routinely gets offered the contact details for people who, in other circumstances, would be justified in calling themselves tall. 'I get crew members coming in,' says Miranda, 'excitedly telling me they have a friend who is six-foot-five. My response is, "Shrimp! Sorry I'm not interested unless they're over six-foot-nine!"'

The tallest person on *The Hobbit* crew is 7'1" Paul Randall (affectionately known as Tall Paul) who, in *The Lord of the Rings*, doubled for Gandalf – as well as several other characters including, it is rumoured, Arwen! Paul now returns to, once again, stand in for Sir Ian McKellen in scenes where Bilbo or the Dwarves need to look the correct size in relation to the wizard.

Liz rattles off some of the other tall characters required for various sequences in the two films: 'We've one tall Legolas, one Radagast, one Beorn, three Gandalfs, two Tauriels…'

'Someday,' Miranda chips in, 'New Zealand's going to run out of tall people!'

Liz's list concludes with: 'Two Silvan Elves and three Elf musicians on harp flute and violin.'

Whatever their height, Elves represent the most demanding of the challenges faced by the Casting Department. Chief requirements? 'Available, tall, slim, line-free, exquisite, androgynous and, preferably, non-annoying individuals.' Ticking all those boxes is not easy. There is, however, one positive aspect to employing the figure-conscious folk who enlist as Elves: when it comes to catering they are, at least, cheap to feed!

Although now much concerned with matters of scale, Liz and Miranda have many memories of the first stages of casting *The Hobbit*, describing the process as 'rather like doing a jigsaw' where all the pieces slowly fit into place.

In line with Peter Jackson's wish to find roles for New Zealand actors, they 'went hell for leather' to get Kiwi and Australian actors to audition. Over 400 actors were considered, some going through multiple auditions until their piece in the jigsaw became clear. With Peter's reputation meaning that he could choose from any actor in the world, the fact that seven of the thirteen Dwarf roles went to local actors is something about which the Casting Department is justifiably proud.

'Even so,' says Miranda, 'we broke a lot of people's hearts including the hundreds of non-actors who love the books and the earlier films and bombarded us with requests to be seen – in just about every language in the world.'

Nowadays, casting requests tend to be more specific, such as a hand-double for Ian Holm needed for a scene where the older Bilbo is writing in a calligraphic script.

'Thanks to modern phones,' says Liz, 'people can now photograph their hands, ears and noses and send them in for consideration. The double body-part business has been totally revolutionized by modern technology!'

OPPOSITE: *Casting Directors Miranda Rivers and Liz Mullane.* TOP: *Hobbit extras, their prosthetic feet protected from dust and dirt, are briefed before preparing to step into Hobbiton.*

Balin

'I read *The Hobbit* as a boy,' says Ken Stott, 'but my father, who was an English teacher, told me *not* to read *The Lord of the Rings*. He said, "You've read *The Hobbit* and that's more than enough Tolkien, now you can move on to something else, like *Crime and Punishment*."'

So, until he started work on this project, Ken was unaware that the name of Balin, the character he is portraying, figures in the book and film of *The Fellowship of the Ring*. While passing through the Mines of Moria, the Fellowship discover Balin's tomb and learn that he was slain by Orcs.

Ken Stott joined the group of actors portraying Thorin's Company of Dwarves from a career that has garnered five Olivier Award nominations. He starred opposite Albert Finney and Tom Courtney in Yasmina Reza's sensationally successful play, *Art*, and originated the role of Michael in Reza's *God of Carnage* on both the London and Broadway stage. Ken has worked with the Royal Shakespeare Company in Stratford-upon-Avon and has appeared in *The Magistrate*, *The Recruiting Officer* and Arthur Miller's *Broken Glass* for the National Theatre of Great Britain. Other stage credits

include *The Faith Healer* and *A View from the Bridge*, while amongst his prolific television work were BAFTA nominated roles in *Hancock and Joan*, *Rebus* and *The Vice*.

Edinburgh-born Ken (like Glasgow-born Graham McTavish, who plays Balin's younger brother, Dwalin) uses his native accent. 'Rather than thinking of us as "Scottish Dwarves", I'd describe it as making use of our accents as a way of delineating the characters and their kinship with one another.'

Talking about the way in which his screen character was defined, Ken says: 'Balin is Thorin's advisor and counsellor. He has been around, he has experience of war and, as a result, we have an opportunity to make him compassionate. In a world that is sword and axe and death and destruction, to be able to search out and portray emotions that are softer, gentler, makes for a good contrast.'

Indeed, juxtaposed with the gung-ho attitude of some of the Dwarves, Balin has some reluctance for the venture. 'We decided that he isn't sure whether it is such a noble idea. That has been a cornerstone for the development of Balin's character in the film. I see his attitude as, "Why are we Dwarves not happy as we are? Must we find more? Why do we want the treasure back? Even though it once belonged to our people, to go and fight for such trinkets is almost tantamount to greed." For many of the Dwarves, the theft of their gold by Smaug the Dragon festers, but for Balin it's all a long time ago and it's gone. Let it be.'

This belief also fires Balin's kindly attitude towards Mr Baggins. 'Basically the Dwarves' feeling about Bilbo is:

"The hobbit is the very last person in whom we ought to be putting our trust! You've only to look at him to know that no one would put money on him getting us through this exploit!" But because of his own reluctance, Balin empathizes with Bilbo's unwillingness to set out on the quest and is able to be more compassionate towards him than some of the others.'

As an actor, Ken believes that the biggest challenge facing members of the Dwarf cast is the prosthetics: 'If they were not so skilfully managed, there might be a danger of losing sight of the person underneath it, but they've avoided that and you can, I think, still tell it's me – which is a relief!'

Like several of the Dwarves, Balin's look went through various changes during pre-production, including the axing of a moustache for the character. 'It just seemed an unnecessary addition,' Ken explains. 'There were two drawings of make-up designs: one with a beard and moustache, one with just the beard. Peter Jackson and I both felt that if you're too busy noticing what's happening on someone's upper lip, then the chances are you'll stop focusing on the eyes, which are essential to conveying character. The moustache was simply one adornment too many and it had to go.'

OPPOSITE: *Balin and his brother, Dwalin (Graham McTavish) wonder what is in Bilbo's pantry.* ABOVE: *Ken Stott, and in costume, showing off Balin's matching beard and boots.*

85

GRAHAM McTAVISH

Dwalin

'With thirteen of us, the internal dynamics of the group are a bit like being back at school: having pretty much got everybody's foibles in our sights, worked out what buttons to press and gauged the limits of everyone's sense of humour, we spend a lot of time making fun of one another!'

Graham McTavish is summing up Thorin's Company of Dwarves whom he refers to as 'The Dirty Baker's Dozen' after the classic 1967 war film, in which a motley bunch of convicts are turned into a crack commando squad and sent on a virtual suicide mission. 'I'm a huge fan of *The Dirty Dozen*,' says Graham, 'and saw the Dwarves as being a bit like the characters in that film. They're an extraordinary group of individuals from different backgrounds with different skills and goals coming together for a single purpose, on an adventure that looks doomed from the outset. But as there are thirteen of us, we are obviously the Dirty *Baker's* Dozen.'

Scottish-born but now living in Los Angeles, Graham played leading roles in British theatre as well as appearing in many television series including *Taggart*, *Casualty* and (appropriately considering his present role) the cult show, *Red Dwarf*. He also played the infamous Russian diplomat, Mikhail Novakovich, in the final season of *24*. Among his films are the 2008 movie *Rambo*, opposite Sylvester Stallone, *Middle Men*, *Secretariat*, *Colombiana* and *The Wicker Tree* (sequel to *The Wicker Man*). He was also the voice of Dante Alighieri in the animated film and video game, *Dante's Inferno*.

Graham has a clear idea of Dwalin's character: 'I decided that Dwalin was an absolute, kick-ass warrior. He's a veteran, professional soldier who lives for fighting and has no illusions about what it's going to be like. Aggressive by nature, he never backs down and he's not big on the jokes. He's not one for cracking the gags around the campfire. Somebody will be telling a great story, but Dwalin's got his axes out and getting those blades nice and sharp.'

There is, Graham believes, a level of Scottishness in the characterization: 'I've met dozens of Dwalins in my native Glasgow – dour, serious folk whom nothing fazes, who are not easily impressed and who tend to keep everyone at arm's length and in their place.'

Nevertheless, Dwalin has strong relationships with Thorin and his own elder brother, Balin: 'Dwalin has a fierce, unbending loyalty to Thorin. There's a bond between them that will never be broken and he will support him as leader even when all the evidence suggests

BELOW: *Dwalin prepares to fly by Eagle; the small red squares are markers that will allow the team at Weta Digital to replace padded claws with real talons.* RIGHT: *Graham McTavish.* FAR RIGHT: *Exploring Bilbo's pantry is thirsty work.*

'I DECIDED THAT DWALIN WAS AN ABSOLUTE, KICK-ASS WARRIOR.'

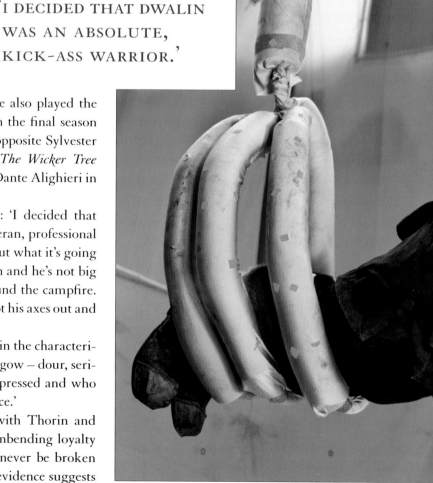

that perhaps he shouldn't. As for Balin, he's the brains and the talker, whereas Dwalin is the brawn and the doer. As I see it, they didn't spend a lot of time with one another as young Dwarves and haven't been together for many years. In working this through, I drew on something of my relationship with my own brother, who is thirteen years older than me and so was always more like an uncle than a brother.'

Graham cuts an impressive figure as Dwalin: with his bald, tattooed head and his huge, muscular forearms. 'To me, the tattoos on my hands, arms and head are a pictorial history of our people, rites of passage, tokens commemorating what has happened to the Dwarven race. As for the forearms, I love them – even if they are made of silicon!'

Unlike his screen character, Graham can be seriously amusing: 'I think of Dwalin as a kind of Hell's Angel of the Dwarf world. You can just imagine him on a massive Harley-Davidson hog bike. In fact, I'm going to call my pony in the movie, Harley: I'll try to slip it in, very briefly, and see if I can get away with it. These are the things that keep me amused. It's quite sad, really!'

Having worked on several Hollywood movies, Graham is aware of the many factors that make *The Hobbit* production unique: 'As actors we have been given so much involvement, like being encouraged to contribute ideas to the design of our characters' weaponry. I remembered having read that the nineteenth-century British novelists, the Brontë sisters, had two dogs called Grasper and Keeper – which are surprising names for a pair of pets. I mentioned this to Peter, in passing, that Grasper and Keeper would be good names for Dwalin's axes – just for me, as a character thing. Peter immediately said, "That's a great idea. We can have them inscribed on the axe blades in Dwarvish." And practically the next day, there they were!'

Reflecting on his time in Middle-earth, Graham says: 'When I was offered this job my reaction was one of complete joy, because I knew that it would be an extraordinary career opportunity. More than that, it's turned out to be an extraordinary *life* opportunity.'

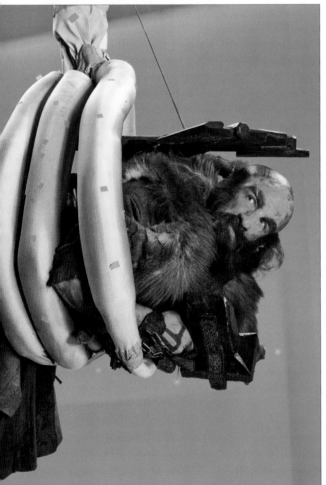

The Return of the Hobbit

The Hobbit turned out to be more than just a one-Bilbo movie. The first Bilbo, played by Martin Freeman, is obviously the story's eponymous hero: Mr Baggins of Bag End, who gets involved with thirteen Dwarves and their quest to recover a lost homeland and stolen treasure.

The *second* Bilbo is the character in later life, with Sir Ian Holm reprising his role from *The Lord of the Rings* and recounting his adventures to his nephew, Frodo. Reflecting on those exploits, Ian Holm says: 'Bilbo is a character to whom things seem to "happen"! But once put to his mettle, once put to the test, he comes up trumps.'

'It's a great way to start the new film,' says Elijah Wood, 'because people who fell in love with *The Lord of the Rings* films will have an easy transition into the world of *The Hobbit* by way of two familiar faces. For me, it was beautiful to share those moments on film with Ian Holm, and it's incredibly appropriate because it helps us understand what made Bilbo the character he is when we meet him in the *Rings* trilogy. It also shows us that the Frodo, whose story we know from those films, is already interested in the outside world – unlike most hobbits – as well as being potentially cut from the same cloth as his uncle.'

Martin Freeman was very conscious of following Ian Holm's performance: I had to remember that he was established from the three other films as a memorable and lovable Bilbo. People adored his portrayal of the character, and I was mindful of that while also being fascinated to discover that the dimensions of our faces are alarmingly similar – although I think my nose may be a bit more of a ski slope than Ian's! I think we make a fairly believable match. Of course, it isn't as if I were playing the young Arnold Schwarzenegger – that *would* be a bit of a stretch!

OPPOSITE: *Martin Freeman plays the younger Bilbo, ready for adventure, and* (ABOVE) *Sir Ian Holm plays the older Bilbo, enjoying a well-earned rest.*

Being in Bag End

'I walked on to set and everyone gave me a round of applause, and Peter came up to me and told me what he wanted me to do, and all I could think is: "Oh, my gosh! This is my first day on my first feature film and I'm in *Bag End*!" It was mind-blowing!' Adam Brown's debut experience as Ori is one shared by all the actors playing the Dwarves, for whom finding themselves on an iconic movie set proved an unforgettable experience.

ABOVE: *Peter and the Dwarves work out how they will all fit in, while Adam Brown (Ori, left) looks on.*
OPPOSITE: *Bilbo hears adventure come knocking.* OVERLEAF: *Peter, Gandalf and the Dwarves decide who is going to do the washing up.*

ABOVE: *Peter, Graham McTavish and Martin Freeman rehearse for a new arrival through a familiar doorway.* BELOW: *Peter and Martin in Bilbo's bedroom, which was newly designed and built for* The Hobbit *and added to the familiar set in Studio B.* OPPOSITE: *A Dwarf's-eye view through Bilbo's front door.*

Graham McTavish, who plays Dwalin, says: 'You can't underestimate the magical effect of finding yourself on a set with which you are so familiar from the earlier films and seeing the incredible attention to detail, most of which is simply glanced at by a camera as it goes by.'

It is a view shared by James Nesbitt, playing Bofur: 'The book is brought to life. Being able to walk into Bag End and appreciate the sheer beauty of the design was just extraordinary. On this one set you see what Peter and everyone involved with this film are so brilliant at doing. By looking at this fabulous world – created such a long time ago, but timeless and universal – through eyes we have as children, it is made totally believable.'

Whatever its charms, being a Dwarf in a hobbit-hole was not without its difficulties. 'On the first day of shooting,' says Richard Armitage, 'the biggest challenge in playing Thorin was getting through the door of Bag End without taking out most of the furniture! Learning how to move around as this character was really difficult because there is *so much of him*! I felt as if I'd stepped into an avatar that I was learning how to control. I really beat myself up about it for the first couple of days because I was feeling really clumsy; and then I thought, "Well actually, maybe that's how Dwarves are when they go into a place where they don't really belong." So I sort of let that go and started to enjoy it.'

Another downside to working in Bag End was the inevitable build-up of heat with so many bodies in heavy costumes and prosthetic make-up cheek-by-jowl in a confined space. Precautions were taken to prevent the cast from

'THEY TOLD US IT WAS GOING TO BE TERRIBLE: HOT, CRAMPED AND DIFFICULT. AND IT *was* HOT – VERY HOT – *and* CRAMPED. BUT IT WASN'T THAT BAD AND WE ALL ENJOYED WHAT WAS A GREAT OPPORTUNITY TO ESTABLISH A KIND OF TOGETHERNESS AS DWARVES.'

overheating, as Adam Brown remembers: 'There were fans underneath the table blowing up our bottoms to keep us cool and there was one day when, I think it's true to say, Mark Hadlow as Dori played the scenes without any trousers on!'

While not confirming this claim, Mark admits that the on-set temperature was somewhat warm: 'It was a bit steamy and uncomfortable, but it was hugely advantageous for our character development because there was nowhere to go. There were all these actors concentrated in that incredible little place, putting in some terrific performances.'

Ken Stott, who plays Balin, agrees: 'They told us it was going to be terrible: hot, cramped and difficult. And it *was* hot – very hot – *and* cramped. But it wasn't that bad and we

all enjoyed what was a great opportunity to establish a kind of togetherness as Dwarves.'

'We were certainly jammed,' recalls Peter Hambleton, playing Gloin. 'Thirteen Dwarves around Bilbo's table *was* a squeeze! And as a result there was some less than gracious behaviour around that table, but you tend to get that whenever you have a bunch of Dwarves together.'

This was ably demonstrated when the lavish hobbit-style meal that Bilbo provides for his unexpected guests rapidly degenerates into a Dwarf food fight that leaves Bag End in chaos. 'We decimated it!' admits Dean O'Gorman, who plays Fili. 'It was a very surreal experience: being on this famous set that we'd all seen from the movies and getting paid to throw food around, knock things over and generally trash the place.'

For Richard, this slapstick introduction to the Dwarves served an important function: 'Something very positive was gained by using scenes involving comedy to establish these characters, who will go on to become heroic, hard-as-nails warriors.'

At the end of two weeks of intense work in Bag End, the cast was left with many memories. For Graham McTavish it is an abiding memory of taking his four-year-old daughter into the small-scale version of Bilbo's home: 'The perfect size for her, it was like the best doll's house a child could ever have. We had to practically drag her out – in fact, she may even still be in there!'

After Gollum

'I've gone over to the Dark Side!' says Second Unit Director, Andy Serkis. 'In terms of a directing debut, this film couldn't possibly be better, but it's not your average first film for a director: it's rather like being given a Ferrari just after you've passed your driving test!'

We are in the caverns under the Misty Mountains where the Dwarves are in the midst of a vicious battle with Goblins. Cordons of hazard-warning tape mark this out as a 'Hot Set', indicating that this rocky warren of passageways is fraught with potential dangers: a combination of seriously uneven surfaces, including rickety plank bridges, blazing torches and open braziers. Not a bad place, perhaps, to be talking to Andy about the pitfalls of moving out of the comfort zone of being an actor into the less-travelled territory of directing other actors.

'It's been amazing,' says Andy of his non-Gollum role on *The Hobbit*. 'But it's also been terrifying – especially in the dark hours in the middle of the night when, maybe, things haven't gone quite as well during the day as I might have liked!'

Of the invitation to work on the film behind the camera, Andy recalls: 'It came totally out of the blue. I arrived here expecting to just do Gollum for a couple of weeks and go home and I've ended up being down here for a year. Pete has known for a long time that I wanted to direct and have been directing short films, video game projects as well as productions for the stage, so it was great to be given this opportunity. However, it's been a sharp learning curve to be working on a feature film and having to come to grips with so many things – not least the challenges of filming in High Definition and 3D.'

The conversation is interrupted by the need for Andy to answer a host of questions from actors, stunt coordinators, cameramen and continuity people. While he is doing that, there's time to reflect on what Peter Jackson says about the man and the task he has undertaken: 'I thought Andy would be an interesting Second Unit Director because he has done all kinds of work, is courageous and will go out on a limb to produce some dynamically interesting footage. To that can be added the fact that our long friendship means that there is trust between us and an easy way of communicating with one another. For me, it is comforting to have someone in that position who is a member of the family.'

'The feeling of family is so important,' says Andy, having answered the demands of his Second Unit crew. 'It is an atmosphere that can't be manufactured. It is borne out of years of people grafting together; people who've evolved, professionally and personally, have an understanding of one

ABOVE: *Andy Serkis, director, sets up a shot in Bag End.*
OPPOSITE: *A younger-looking Gollum, with hair.*

another's talents, and are able to dovetail their skills and abilities together into a tight-knit and really efficient unit.'

The years of working on Jackson projects have provided a degree of preparation. 'First and foremost,' says Andy, 'Peter is concerned with creativity and great ideas. There's no sense of hierarchy; if anyone in the cast or crew came up with an idea that was gold, Peter will embrace it. He *is* exacting: he demands a hundred-and-fifty per cent. He always has and he probably always will. But the level of commitment he receives is phenomenal because his own commitment filters down to everyone involved. The expectation may be for a hundred-and-fifty per cent, but so is the sense of your worth and value. That's not something you routinely get on projects of this size.'

Everyone breaks for lunch and, as we leave the Goblin Caverns, one of the Dwarves, Mark Hadlow, offers an actor's perspective on the Second Unit Director: 'Andy is an amazing actor, but although not all good actors make good directors Andy absolutely *does*. There's so much talent wrapped up in this one individual and I am insanely jealous of him! What makes matters worse is he's not just talented, he's also a nice person! It's just not fair!'

OPPOSITE: *(Above) Andy Serkis, director, in front of the camera for a behind-the-scenes video. (Below) Trying on Thorin's Oakenshield.* TOP: *Planning the next scene with Director of Photography, 2nd Unit, Richard Bluck.*

MARK HADLOW

Dori

Being intimately associated with a hippo named Heidi who got herself nominated as Best Actress in the New Zealand Film Awards is, perhaps, an unlikely claim to fame, but one that Mark Hadlow, now playing Dori, proudly acknowledges. A diva among hippos, Heidi starred in the 1989 puppet splatter movie, *Meet the Feebles*. Her voice – along with those for Roger the Hedgehog and Barry the Bulldog – was provided by Mark, working for the first time with director, Peter Jackson. 'I knew back then,' he says, 'that there was something quite extraordinary about Peter and his team of filmmakers; something interesting, exciting and inspirational.'

Mark is acutely aware of the differences between the circumstances under which *Feebles* was filmed, twenty-three years ago, in a damp, dirty, draughty, flea-infested railway shed and the sophisticated studio set-up and luxurious actors' trailers being enjoyed on *The Hobbit*. 'It is a direct result of Peter's talent, guts, determination and sheer bloody mindedness to have started with nothing and to now be masterminding what is, at the moment, the greatest film project in the world.'

However, some things, Mark says, have not changed over the years: 'With many film projects there seem to be all kinds of issues, but you never seem to see those when you're working on a Jackson film. You just have a whole heap of fun, and that scares me a bit because it's supposed to be *work*!'

Mark played Harry, a struggling vaudevillian in the early scenes of Peter Jackson's *King Kong* and appeared in the 2008 Kiwi comedy-zombie movie, *Last of the Living*, but is best known in New Zealand for his extensive stage work and for television series such as *Willy Nilly* and *The Billy T James Show*.

He is one of seven native New Zealanders to be cast in the company of Dwarves: 'I think it's a stroke of genius on Peter's part to cast seven Kiwis as Dwarves, giving us the chance to work alongside six brilliant British actors without our ever feeling we are the "B" team; instead we are all part of the same "A" team. To me that's amazing!'

'THE DWARVES ARE A SERIES OF CLANS AND THEIR CLANNISHNESS IS VITAL TO THE WAY IN WHICH THEIR CHARACTERS DEVELOP.'

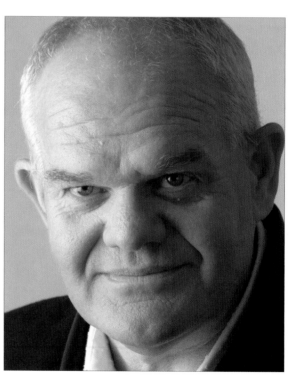

ABOVE: *Mark Hadlow.* RIGHT: *Three brothers: Nori, Dori and Ori.*

Mark first read *The Hobbit* as a ten-year-old, and enjoyed what he calls the book's 'Boys' Own Adventure' qualities. But he admits to missing the presence in Middle-earth of the Second World War Spitfires that featured in his favourite childhood reading! Coming back to Tolkien's story as an adult meant finding and understanding the character he had been cast to play.

'As Dori,' he says, 'I am the eldest and in the prime of my youth. I've got two younger brothers, Nori, and Ori, who is, in Dwarf-years, a mere teenager! There is a powerfully strong sense of family: I care more than anything about young Ori and I worry about Nori, who's a bit of a vagabond and the black sheep of the family. They are like the Middle-earth version of a working-class family: tight-knit, fiercely loyal, warm and friendly but if you cross them – they'll kill you! It's important for me, as an actor, to keep this sense of family visible throughout the movie so that we are clearly seen as a group that grows and gets stronger and more emotionally connected.'

For Mark, these allegiances lie at the heart of the story: 'The Dwarves are a series of clans and their clannishness is vital to the way in which their characters develop. It is something we've worked at as a group of actors, establishing the various bonds and rivalries that exist between and within those clans.'

Mark is particularly fond of Peter Jackson's personal name for the group: 'He calls us "the little b******s"! It's such a term of endearment! Peter is an extraordinary man and, you know, there are no airs or graces with him; he's set up this nice, easy, jovial way of working: "Ah, you little b******s," he'll say, "let's get into it and do it!" Peter is incredibly gifted at being able to get actors to put aside their personal egos and just get on with giving some really great performances.'

Mark's excitement to be one of Dwarves in *The Hobbit* is unquenchable: 'I've been acting for thirty-three years and I'm part of this extraordinary tale. It's a quest into fantasyland: I come into the studio every day and we do this amazing stuff! What's more, we've seen the prototypes of how our images as characters will be reproduced on merchandise. I love it: there's going to be an actual action figure made of my character! I mean, Christmas is taken care of for the next ten years!'

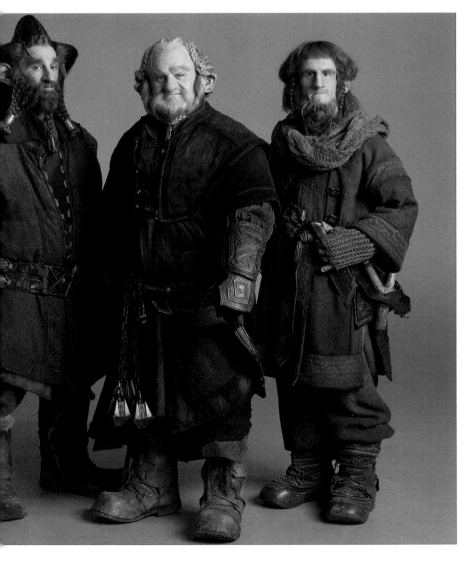

ABOVE: *With hair, prosthetic make-up and beard in place, Mark is dressed in layer after layer of costume, as he is gradually transformed into Dori in one of the Production's Wardrobe tents.*

JED BROPHY

Nori

'**W**hat's mine is mine and what's yours is mine – and you're not getting it back!' That's Jed Brophy's one-line description of the character of Nori.

Jed is a hugely experienced New Zealand actor with award-winning theatre productions (*Skin Tight*, which he co-devised, won a Fringe First at the Edinburgh Festival) and countless short films and television credits. He has also appeared in numerous feature films, among them *Second Hand Wedding*, *Warrior's Way* and the cult SF film, *District 9*, as well as six Peter Jackson movies, starting twenty years ago in 1992 with *Braindead* and going on to include *Heavenly Creatures*, *King Kong* and *The Lord of the Rings* trilogy, in which he portrayed assorted denizens of Middle-earth. 'I've played Men, Elves, Orcs (such as Snaga and Sharku), Uruk-hai and Ringwraiths. I think the only creatures I've not represented are Trolls, hobbits and, until *now*, Dwarves. In fact, I'd never, in a million years, thought that I was the right physical type to play a Dwarf.'

The decision to cast the company of Dwarves as varied, rather than uniform, physical types made it possible for Jed to tick off another of the Middle-earth races. Although taking on a Dwarven persona involved a good deal of creativity, as he explains: 'I've got a narrow face, so to make me seem bigger in the head, I've got this massive, three-piece Mohawk hair-do and a lot of beardage making my face appear larger. But, apart from the look, the challenge is to play characters who are not human, but have a lot of human characteristics. You have to balance this with an understanding of what it is that makes the Dwarves identifiable as a separate race, and ask: how would a Dwarf, knowing the history of his people, react to a situation?'

Ask Jed to describe the character of Nori and the epithets come thick and fast: 'He's very vain and he's a bit dodgy: an outsider, a wide-boy, a schemer, a wheeler-dealer

and a kleptomaniac – well, let's not mince words, a *thief*! Ostracized by his family, he's been living rough, on his own, in the wild (which is amazing considering his great hair-do!); he won't take a backward step from anyone and no matter how big the creature that comes up against him, he'll have a crack at fighting it. Lovely guy though, but probably not someone who you'd want marrying your daughter!'

While Jed is steeped in Tolkien's writings about the history of Middle-earth, it is, he says, largely a closed book to Nori: 'He is not sure about Thorin regaining his lost kingdom – the idea of a Dwarf King doesn't excite him because

OPPOSITE: *Nori enjoys the Elven cuisine, while eyeing up the fine candelabra.* LEFT: *Jed Brophy.* BELOW: *Exploring Trollshaw Forest.*

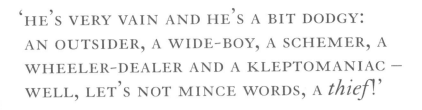

no Dwarf King has ever done anything for him – he just wants his share of the treasure and anybody else's he can get his hands on. Despite being part of the group, he has his own agenda and that's looking out for Number One.'

Nori, says Jed, has a difficult relationship with his family: 'Nori is the middle child, looked down on by Dori, the elder brother, and looked up to by Ori, the younger one. Dori acts like the parent of the family, wanting to be in charge and treating the other two as lesser beings and Nori really doesn't like that. So he listens to Dori, but he doesn't really *listen*, if you know what I mean.'

Personal relationships aren't really Nori's strong suit: 'There's a lot of antagonism between him and Dwalin and, as far as Bilbo Baggins is concerned, he cannot understand why he has been chosen for the job of burglar. Nori is a thief and there is a saying: set a thief to catch a thief, meaning that one thief can always identify another. Nori is not convinced that Bilbo's particularly good as a thief – especially since he's managed to take some stuff from Bag End that Bilbo hasn't even noticed has gone missing! Apart from which, why employ a thief at all when there's already one in the company?'

Along with other Kiwi actors, Jed had been involved in the 'pre-visualization' (or pre-viz) of *The Hobbit*, in which the script is filmed as a storyboard with actors' voices, so that Peter Jackson can advance-plan how the film will be shot. To then be invited to play one of the central characters was an unexpected bonus. 'When my agent rang me,' Jed remembers, 'I was at home alone and went from whooping great whoops of delight to weeping tears of joy. *The Hobbit* was the first book I remember reading, when I was seven years old, so to be part of something this grand was, I can safely say, the most thrilling moment of my career. And I'm *still* excited about it!'

Ori

'Do you know what I like most about Ori?' asks Adam Brown, who makes his film debut in *The Hobbit*. 'The fact that he is so naïve and innocent. When we all become little toys, I won't be a bit surprised if he's the one that gets left in the toy box by the boys and ends up being played with by their sisters and kept in their doll's houses!'

An experienced comedy performer and one half of the successful theatre company, Plested and Brown, Adam got a call from his agent saying that he was being asked to try out for *The Hobbit*. Assuming it was for a touring stage production and not relishing the thought of months on the road, he said he'd rather not. 'My agent said, "*No!* We're talking Peter Jackson's *film* of *The Hobbit*!" So, obviously, I went!'

Adam recorded a video audition for the role of Bilbo. 'I knew I wasn't a Bilbo, but word came back that they'd really liked what I'd done and were looking for a role for me. I thought I might get third-villager-from-the-left but, eight weeks later, I was offered the part of Ori.'

He got the news when he was in a car driving through north London in appalling weather. 'I didn't believe it at first, and then I did a lot screaming and shouting! I stopped at a pub and went and had a Scotch – it may have been *two*, actually, and I *never* drink whiskey. I wanted to share the news with people but my mobile phone was dead, so I was wandering round the pub desperately asking if anyone had a phone-charger!'

Only later did Adam discover that the screenwriters were going to base Ori's screen persona on his audition. 'I love the fact that Ori has been built on my performance,' he says. 'I was pretty petrified when I auditioned and that's what must have been what came over! There's a good bit of me in the character, although I don't think I'm quite as nerdy as Ori!'

Adam really enjoys talking about Ori's character: 'He's a fish out of water, a little boy lost; he's very intelligent and really quite sensitive (he probably also has a nut allergy) but even though he's not macho like the other Dwarves, he is really up for going on this journey. He's rather like a raw, young army recruit: keen, wet behind the ears and with absolutely no idea what he's getting into.'

Ori is unlike his fellow travelling companions in just about every respect, as Adam explains: 'All the other Dwarves wear lots of leather and metal, but Ori's got a knitted cardigan and little mittens; and while they're all equipped with swords and axes, all he has is a tiny catapult. Not only that, but they all have big beards, while I have a very small one and a moustache, which is barely noticeable. I had to guzzle a big mug of ale in Bag End and my moustache came off in the beer and I swallowed it!'

> 'I DIDN'T BELIEVE IT AT FIRST,
> AND THEN I DID A LOT SCREAMING
> AND SHOUTING! I STOPPED AT A PUB
> AND WENT AND HAD A SCOTCH.'

It is likely that Ori is going to mature as the journey progresses and there is already a serious side to his character as he is the group's scribe: 'I've had calligraphy lessons,' says Adam, 'and Ori carries a book in which he is always recording events and making sketches.' This duty was given to Ori in acknowledgement that in part one of *The Lord of the Rings*, the Fellowship passing under the Misty Mountains find the Book of Mazarbul in which Ori had recoded the last stand of Balin and his company against the Orcs of Moria. The scene was depicted in *The Fellowship of the Ring* film with the Book still in the clutches of Ori's crumbling remains. 'I did a cracking job in that movie,' jokes Adam. 'I lost a lot of weight for that role: practically a skeleton!'

Speaking about Ori's siblings, Dori and Nori, Adam says: 'As we've figured it out, the three brothers share a mother in common but have different fathers. That would explain our individual characteristics. Dori is like an old mother hen to poor Ori, constantly pecking at his shoulder, going, "Have you eaten your greens? Tidy up! Do your button up or you'll get cold." Nori is the trickster, the wild card, the rebel without a cause who's hardly ever around because he's off causing mischief; then he bursts in on their lives, causes a kerfuffle and disappears again. Ori wishes he were a bit

OPPOSITE: *Dori, Fili, Nori and Ori enjoy Bilbo's hospitality.*
ABOVE: *Ori, the fearsome Dwarf warrior...*

more adventurous like Nori, which is why he follows him on the quest, while Dori just wants to try and get him safely back home. We all end up going together, fiercely loyal to one another while bickering and arguing most of the time.'

Reflecting on Ori and his own involvement in *The Hobbit*, Adam says: 'Out of everybody on this Quest, I think Ori has the biggest journey to make. And for me that means making him someone who is different and likeable. These films are going to stay on the DVD shelves for a long time. So, I really need to get it right!'

A Deeply Distressing Job

'**P**eople think that costume breakdown is just about making clothes look filthy, but it's about much more than that.' Amy Wright's title is Key Breakdown Artist and she and her team are responsible for taking the newly finished costumes and making them look as if the characters have *worn* them – possibly for a very long time.

'When costumes reach us,' says Amy, 'they have been beautifully made out of wonderful fabrics, often exquisitely embroidered and, quite a lot of the time, we then set about destroying them!'

Whether a garment is to be wrecked or just made to look loved and lived in, the one thing it mustn't look is *new*. Or to put it another way, it really mustn't look like a 'costume'.

Amy's criterion for what it takes to be a successful breakdown artist is twofold: 'You need to be a creative person who is good at problem solving. Additionally, you need an eye for composition and use of colour because, as much as anything else, breakdown is about using colour to age a garment.'

Of the many challenges in the breakdown process being solved today is a possible costume option for a piece of leather armour for Legolas, which is being painted to give it varying patinas of green and copper tones.

'Each costume is unique in how we deal with it,' Amy explains. 'Because every costume has a different fabric and a different story to tell, we have to use a variety of tools and equipment.'

These include sandpaper for rubbing the shine off items, wire brushes for making wool and other materials look snagged and pulled, and a vicious-looking gadget called a rasper, which is particularly useful for giving leather a roughed-up look.

So how do the breakdown artists avoid doing the same to their hands? 'You just do it the once,' says Amy, 'and then never again!'

Other useful implements include airbrushes, blow-torches, heat guns and a variety of jeweller's tools, including miniature sanders for getting into tight corners and taking the edge off edges.

One of Amy's team, Costume Art Finisher, Hamish Brown, is currently using a pair of eyebrow tweezers to painstakingly pick the pile off parts of Bilbo's burgundy coloured corduroy travelling jacket, in order to make it look worn where the straps of his backpack would have rubbed at the material. 'At every stage of the journey, Bilbo has a different coat, each more worn than the last. This is a fifth-stage jacket and I am copying the pattern of worn pile from the one worn by Martin Freeman onto one that will be worn by his stunt-double; even though it may only be shot from a helicopter, I am still being quite fastidious.'

This is the twelfth Bilbo jacket that Hamish has pile-picked and he admits that staying sane is sometimes a challenge. 'In fact,' he admits, 'we *do* go a bit crazy. But it's a kind of controlled craziness and, I think, if you're not a little crazy you're probably not doing the job right.'

Hamish is wearing a rather natty waistcoat that is the costume destined to be worn by a Hobbiton resident named Gammidge. 'The best way to make a costume look worn,' he explains, 'is to wear it. That way, you get the creases and folds where the body puts them.'

But when it comes to a costume such as that for Radagast, where the character is supposed to have been wearing it for many years, how do they know when they have done enough breaking down, when it is time to stop? Amy and Hamish admit that sometimes they don't, but those are rare occasions.

'If you make a mistake and go too far,' says Amy, 'you'd have to start again with a new costume, but there's absolutely never any time to start again. So, the best advice is: jump in there and go for it! Don't be afraid!'

'But,' adds Hamish, 'you should always have your bags packed – just in case!'

OPPOSITE: *Sylvester McCoy, not looking as distressed as his costume.* ABOVE: *Having escaped from Goblin Town, the Dwarves' costumes need to show wear and tear as well as mud-stains. Peter checks that they are now ready to climb some pine-trees.*

Dwarf-mess, Goblin-blood & Troll-snot

Ask the Costume Breakdown team what have been the most challenging things that have been demanded of them and it is a question they find difficult to answer, mainly because strange and bizarre requests are pretty much a daily occurrence. Amy Wright suggests it might be the need to apply food stains to the clothes of someone who is a messy eater (you can't use real food because it would become smelly) to various kinds of blood – there are, it seems, different recipes depending on whether the blood is dried or runny, and most of them use paint mixed with glycerines, glues and pastes to give different consistencies.

Amy's colleague, Hamish, opts for the scene in which Bilbo and the Dwarves encounter the three Trolls: one of them violently sneezes on Bilbo, covering him in what can only be described as Troll-snot!

'It's one of the problems with fantasy films,' laughs Hamish. 'You have to keep things looking believable but at the same time you are dealing with a hobbit smothered in the contents of a Troll's nose!'

ABOVE: *Martin patiently allows himself to be covered in slime.*
RIGHT: *Bilbo stares up at the creature that used him as a handkerchief.*

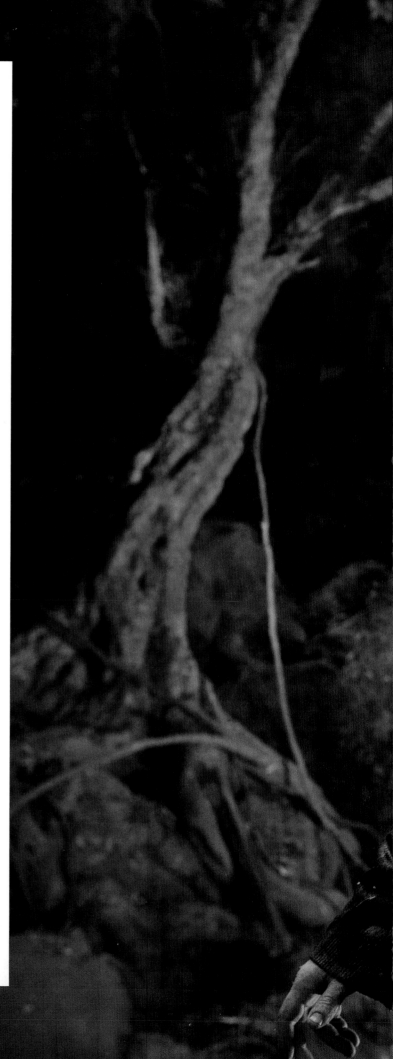

OIN

'If an actor can't surprise himself or herself, then they're not going to surprise the audience. And if we're not offering surprises to the audience, it's all a bit bland really, isn't it?'

John Callen, who plays Oin, speaks from experience: the oldest member of the Dwarf cast is one of New Zealand's most prolific actors and directors with over one hundred theatre credits, among them such major Shakespearian roles as Macbeth and Shylock, as well as lecturing drama and appearing in and directing many hours of TV series, documentaries and commercials. His films include *Love Birds*, *The Man Who Lost His Head* with Martin Clunes and *The Sinking of the Rainbow Warrior* with John Voight and Sam Neill.

Approaching the age of 65 and about to relinquish his teaching engagement at Auckland University, John told his agent that he needed her to find him a job that would set him up for his retirement. She laughed. The following day, the agent rang and asked John if he was sitting down… When he did (he had been vacuuming dog hairs off the sofa when the phone rang) he was told he had been offered the role of Oin.

'Being employed for the best part of two years,' says John, 'is an exceptional chunk of work for an actor in New Zealand – or an actor anywhere, come to that. And this is an exceptional job to be doing.'

John had auditioned for *The Hobbit*, but for two other roles: Radagast the Brown and the voice of Smaug the Dragon, so he knew very little about the part he had just won. After reading Tolkien's novel, John says, he didn't feel much the wiser: 'Oin is relatively thinly drawn in the book and there's two ways of looking at that: you either say, "Crikey, we've got nothing to work with!" or "Crikey, we've got *carte blanche*!"'

From Tolkien came the fact that, with his brother Gloin, he is a firelighter, responsible for the Dwarves' campfires. Oin was then developed into an apothecary, or herbalist, who travels with a bag of early medical instruments and bottles containing various concoctions. 'In fact,' jokes John, 'I would like to think that Oin was, perhaps, the inventor of *oin*tment!'

John is full of praise for the way in which the *Hobbit* scripts have developed the story and the characters. 'At the beginning of the film, the audience will view the Dwarves as being just a bunch of naughty boys and will fall in love with them as a group and as individuals. Then, once we get past all the boyish tomfoolery and serious things start happening, they will have already made an emotional investment in them as characters and care about them and want them to succeed. That is very good storytelling.'

As Oin's character was refined, it was decided that he should be somewhat deaf. 'He tends to mishear things,' explains John, 'and is not quite so quick on the uptake as the others, because although he's perfectly intelligent he doesn't necessarily hear what's going on – such as being charged at by the enemy!'

Fitting Footwear for Dwarves

'As an actor,' says John Callen, 'the shoes are the most important part of any costume. What I wear on my feet determines how I walk and that is a vital factor in deciding how I play my character.'

Working out what the Dwarves were going to wear on their feet involved a great deal of research and development. 'What we needed,' says Costume Designer, Ann Maskrey, 'was something that looked right but was light enough for the actors to walk in – without tripping over.'

The solution was shoes the right size for the actor built into a solid-looking Dwarf boot. Movement choreographer, Terry Notary, tested the footwear and demonstrated that they would work with the rolling gait of the Dwarves.

Lighter-weight versions were, subsequently, made to be used on the more demanding terrain found on location, but most of the actors preferred the heavier boots as a way of mastering the art of becoming a Dwarf.

It certainly worked for John Callen. 'As soon as the boots went on,' he says, 'everything clicked!'

OPPOSITE: *Oin uses his ear-trumpet to listen to the others.* LEFT: *Oin proudly displays his boots and* (INSET) *John Callen.*

Oin also has a taste for red wine – eight to a dozen glasses at a time. 'That,' says John with mock seriousness, 'is, as you can imagine, a characteristic that is incredibly difficult to act convincingly.'

Playing a Dwarf involves serious dedication to the actor's craft, as John quickly discovered. The costume, hair and prosthetic make-up added twenty-eight kilos to his bodyweight. He also quickly discovered that what he imagined would be an asset to playing the character – his own long white hair and beard – were going to add considerably to the time he would have to spend in the make-up chair. A drastic haircut and shave quickly followed.

As for the replacement whiskers that are daily applied, they brought their own problems: 'I frequently find that, at lunchtime, I am eating yak hair, which is not as tasty as the food they serve us! There have also been a couple of occasions when a few oddments of lunch have remained *in the beard*, but that doesn't matter too much because these Dwarves have pretty bad table manners.'

John spent time with Peter Hambleton, who plays Gloin, in dreaming up ideas about the siblings' past history. Knowing that apothecaries used to act as midwives, they came up with a theory: 'We thought that if, maybe, Oin had assisted at the birth of his nephew, Gimli, and had unfortunately dropped the baby on its head, it might account for some of the weirder things that Gimli does and says in *The Lord of the Rings*!'

Gloin

'**G**loin and his brother, Oin, are related to Thorin, but although we've connections with royalty, you could say that, basically, we're middle-management in the Dwarf realm.'

Peter Hambleton, who plays Gloin, is a multi award-winning actor and director with numerous stage and TV credits and is a native New Zealander, born and bred in Wellington. 'I've lived in this city all my life and this extraordinary set-up here at the studio has been on my own doorstep for a number of years; and now I'm working for it!'

Along with several other Kiwi actors, Peter auditioned in 2010, but without any expectations of getting a leading role: 'I've not done a lot of film work, so I didn't get my hopes up. I gave the audition my best shot, but I thought what was more likely was that one or two of the smaller parts might come our way like a few crumbs falling from the table.'

In the event, Peter's agent rang to say that he was being offered the role of Gloin. 'I didn't believe him,' he recalls. 'It was the most amazing opportunity to have fall in your lap, out

of the blue. I still have to pinch myself every day to believe it!'

Although he hadn't previously appeared in a Jackson film, Peter was one of a group of local actors filming motion-capture (mocap) footage for the Spielberg-Jackson production, *The Adventures of Tintin: The Secret of the Unicorn*. 'I had a day-long session with Peter playing a variety of characters and I suppose he had the opportunity to see what I was capable of, because when I got the part Peter told me that my mocap work had been a kind of extended audition.'

How does Peter Hambleton see the character of Gloin? 'His default setting is angry: he's a prickly customer and a bit of a grump and that's where the fun lies in terms of his role in the story. But he also has a passion for what the Dwarves must achieve, a sense of the rightness of the mission they're on and, like all of them, is prepared to give his all to achieve it.'

Gloin's character was developed and eventually defined through discussions with Peter Jackson, Fran Walsh and Philippa Boyens. 'It was a fun, collaborative process,' says Peter Hambleton. 'Gloin is the father of Gimli, so audiences might notice recognizable characteristics such as his feisty, aggressive temperament and a tendency to take umbrage.'

Gloin shares more than just personality traits with his son, there is also the look: 'The red hair, the big bushy beard, the accent (a kind of Middle-earth form of Scottish!) will feel familiar, as will the axe he carries, which is the weapon that will later pass from father to son and be used by Gimli in *Rings*.'

Discussions on the development of Gloin's character led to some interesting new perspectives on the Quest to recover the lost treasure of the Dwarves: 'We decided that Gloin looks after the finances – a sort of Dwarf accountant – and has possibly been involved in putting together the funding for the mission.'

Peter admits that some Dwarven attributes are less attractive than others, particularly their fondness for food fights. 'We Dwarves see it as part of our culture and think we've taken the art to the absolute peak of perfection. Who knows, it might even start a trend for international food fight tournaments.'

Like several members of the cast, Peter is still coming to terms with the fact that he is in a film that has all the indications of being a guaranteed blockbuster. 'I'm learning every day just how life-transforming this is going to be. It is an extraordinary, fantastic opportunity for me, because I've been working as a professional theatre actor for close on thirty years, doing my best to survive in a very small place. Then suddenly a few things line up and I'm now learning a whole bunch of new skills, discovering how a different industry operates and working on one of the biggest film projects ever made!'

If what happened to those involved in *The Lord of the Rings* trilogy is anything to go by, Peter Hambleton, along with all the New Zealand actors in the cast, will soon be enjoying international celebrity. 'In terms of make-up,' he says, 'I am very much down the Dwarven end of the spectrum, so I don't really expect people to recognize me after the film comes out, but this is such unknown territory to me that I've really no idea. Since I can't entirely take it in, I don't worry about it; I just concentrate on enjoying the experience and absolutely savouring every day.'

OPPOSITE: *Andy Serkis directs Peter, Aidan and James Nesbitt as they prepare to rescue Bilbo from the Trolls, one of whose 'legs' can be seen behind Andy.* ABOVE: *Gloin carries the axe he will hand on to his son, Gimli. Peter Hambleton.*

TERRY NOTARY, MOVEMENT CHOREOGRAPHER

The Notable Mr Notary

How does a Dwarf walk? Or an Elf, or a hobbit? The man to ask is Movement Choreographer, Terry Notary.

A former championship gymnast, Terry spent five years as an acrobat with Cirque du Soleil and worked with the Metropolitan Opera before moving into film, providing movement coaching for the Whos of Whoville in *How the Grinch Stole Christmas* and doing stunts for Tim Burton's *Planet of the Apes*. Other films on which he worked include *The Incredible Hulk*, *Avatar*, and with Andy Serkis on *Rise of Planet of the Apes* and *The Adventures of Tintin: The Secret of the Unicorn*, which also brought him into contact with Peter Jackson and earned him an invitation to join the team on *The Hobbit*.

'I am a huge fan of *The Lord of the Rings*,' says Terry, 'and whenever I watched the film trilogy, I'd think, how much I wished I had been able to be involved in them, so I am hugely excited to be working with Peter Jackson and the actors to use movement as a way of representing the different races of Middle-earth.'

Terry's movement exercises always begin with an image: 'I give each actor a mental picture. I ask them what it is that drives their character. If their body were a vehicle or a machine what would be the fuel that would make it operate? It might be oil or water, air or fire or, even, bile. This kind of exercise gives an actor the confidence of feeling that they have a set of rules – although they are very flexible rules – that provide a foundation for understanding their character.'

RIGHT: *Terry Notary (right) coaches one of the stunt performers, dressed in full motion-capture suit, to move like a Goblin.*

'WHAT I AM TEACHING IS MORE ABOUT UNDERSTANDING HOW TO BE STILL AND YET, AT THE SAME TIME, KEEP THE CHARACTER ALIVE AND HAVE THE CONFIDENCE TO KNOW THAT YOU CAN INSTANTLY SPRING FROM THAT NEUTRAL POSITION INTO ACTION.'

An example of one of Terry's exercises to help the actors playing Elves to understand how to walk would be to ask them to imagine that they are not moving by themselves but are being wrapped up and carried along by the wind. Then he will give them another image for when they have to stop moving: 'It mustn't look sudden or abrupt; what happens to the physical energy of walking when Elves come to a standstill should be like what would happen if you squirted ink into water – it would dissipate and dissolve away.'

So, how do the actors react to such exercises? 'One or two are, maybe, a bit sceptical at first,' admits Terry, 'but, sooner or later, they embrace the ideas. And most of them find it really helpful and love it.'

Though part of Terry's job description is 'Movement Coach', in many ways he is 'a stillness coach' as he explains: 'What I am teaching is more about understanding how to be still and yet, at the same time, keep the character alive and have the confidence to know that you can instantly spring from that neutral position into action.'

The process of devising these ideas begins for Terry with long, solitary walks, usually along a beach. 'Planning moves always starts with a shape. For example, in the case of a Goblin, that shape would be a crumpled piece of paper. It has a lot of sharp angles and little curves and broken lines of energy, and it has no foundation so it doesn't sit on the ground with weight; but it's very agile and resilient, so it's easy to knock away, but it always rolls right back.'

One of the drawbacks to his work is that Terry is unable to stop the process of analyzing movement. 'It is,' he says, 'almost like a curse: I am unconsciously watching how people walk, how an animal runs, how a bird takes off or lands. It's almost a monstrous obsession; I just can't turn it off! But it is great fun to gather all sorts of ideas from different inspirations and piece them together in order to create something that is completely unique. Every day is a new experience, a new challenge – all I have to do is keep up with the monster!'

Notary's Notes

❖

On Dwarves

'The Dwarves, like hobbits, are of the earth. They follow their gut-reactions and act on instinct, but because they carry a great burden – the weight of history that sits like a great chip on their shoulders – they leave a massive footprint behind, so you know that they've been there.

'It's important that the audience can relate to the characters that are the heroes of the piece. We need to be able to feel that they march to the same beat as ourselves. The Dwarves' movements follow a time signature of a four-count: '*Bom-Bom-Bom-Bom, Bom-Bom-Bom-Bom*', and when, as a group, they come to stop, there is a sense of completion.

'Although they are short of stature, they don't feel the need to be tall and they don't have to puff themselves up in order to be tough. They have an iron core and cruise through the terrain like miniature tanks. But contrasting with the strength and toughness is a good, light sense of humour that always comes shining through.'

On hobbits

'Hobbits are grounded, they are connected to the earth, so there's stability to them, but there is also lightness and bounce. They are like little bouncing electrons or sparkling water.

'They are a bit like moles in that they live underground but they also have this sense of intrigue and inquisitiveness.

'Hobbits have a constant bubble that you might think of as being three-steps-forward-and-one-step-back. They are gentle and sprightly and they are constantly second-guessing, checking things out, darting from one idea to another.'

ON ELVES

'Elves have an amazing synergy with nature; they ebb and flow like a piece of seaweed in the ocean.

'They move, in a way, like a wind that passes through the trees and disappears: it comes and goes. Their movements are very simple but uniquely beautiful and graceful at the same time.

'Elves also have an innate poise without ever posturing. Imagine you are seeing a famous ballet dancer across the room at a cocktail party. She is not dancing, she is just standing there with a glass in her hand, relaxed and totally unaware of her beauty; but the grace and posture that make her a great dancer are there as part of her. That's exactly what the Elves have and it is something they are born with.

'If you are playing an Elf, everything is very simple but very complex, because your outward appearance has to come from what is inside. It's as if the Elves have to look inward to see out. They see with a soft focus, they're not focused on one thing at one time, they don't dart from thought to thought; instead, they see the whole picture, the whole world all at once as if they can see how everything comes together into a single source of energy.'

PETER KING, MAKE-UP & HAIR DESIGNER

Hair-raising Tales from Middle-earth

'**I** was calmly told they needed wigs for six tall-scale Silvan Elves by tomorrow. So, I asked them: "Where do you think they are coming from? All the wig-trees are bare! We have plucked them all!"'

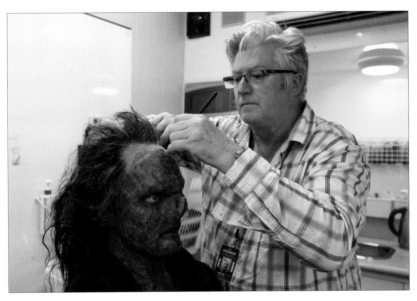

Peter King, *The Hobbit*'s flamboyant Make-Up and Hair Designer, is jesting about the sort of pressures that he and his 42-person team have to confront and overcome on a daily basis.

Peter, who won two Oscars and a BAFTA for his work on the *Rings* trilogy, has an impressive pedigree. He designed the make-up for Andrew Lloyd Webber's globally successful stage musical, *The Phantom of the Opera*, while his film credits include an eclectic string of movies from *The Portrait of a Lady* and *Miss Julie* to *Velvet Goldmine* and *Quills*. In addition to the Jackson *Rings* cycle and *King Kong*, Peter's recent films include *Beyond the Sea*, *The Golden Compass*, Francis Ford Coppola's *Youth Without Youth*, Rob Marshall's *9* and two *Nanny McPhee* movies.

It was while completing work on *Pirates of the Caribbean 4* that Peter first heard that a new Jackson project was getting underway, when he got an email from Producer and 1st Assistant Director, Carolynne Cunningham: 'She wrote that they were making a little film called *The Hobbit* and that it was going to be much smaller than *Rings* – only two films – and would I like to go and play? I re-read the book and thought: "Hang on! It's about thirteen Dwarves! What does she mean, 'a *little* film'?"'

OPPOSITE: *The exquisite detailing of the wigs means they will look real even when filmed in HD.* TOP: *Peter King at work on an Orc hair-do.* LEFT: *Some of the hundreds of extras' wigs are prepared ready to be applied.*

'In the book,' says Peter, 'Tolkien mentions that several of the Dwarves have different coloured beards tucked into their belts – blue, red, yellow and white – so before coming to New Zealand, I experimented with various coloured hair samples, using natural tones, such as an earthy red, that would look subtle rather than outlandish. Happily, when I arrived, I found that the idea of coloured beards had already been abandoned.'

There was, however, a vast quantity of concept art initiated by Weta Workshop: 'Quite often, design concepts are as useful for showing what you *don't* want something to look like as what it *should* look like. It was an intensely collaborative process, but thirteen characters took a lot of discussing and, after six weeks of deliberations, I finally said, "We're going to have to stop talking about wigs and beards and start making them!"'

The hair worn on everyone's heads and faces is made in Britain by the same craftspeople who worked on *Rings* – wigs by Peter King's former colleague, Oscar-winning Peter Owen of Bristol, and beards by Sarah Weatherburn of London. They have a crucial role to play in helping regular human actors appear to be Dwarves.

'Having a lot of elaborate plaited hair,' explains Peter, 'assists in making their heads look bigger, while the huge beards hide the actors' necks and make their bodies appear squatter. The rest of the design is about creating the feeling of a band of characters each with a distinct and individual personality.'

It proved a valid question: the reality is that those thirteen characters each require two sets of wigs and beards, and have an assortment of doubles for shots involving characters of different scales or for special types of action such as riding and stunts. At the last count, Peter King's department was managing no fewer than 91 wigs and beards for the Dwarves alone – before they even start thinking about what is needed for hobbits, Elves and wizards.

'With the exception of one or two extras,' says Peter, 'every character in the movie has a wig or a wig and a beard. We even have some Dwarf women and children and they have beards, too!'

The individual hairstyles and whiskers worn by Thorin's Company of Dwarves was the end product of a great deal of pre-production thinking.

ABOVE: *Richard Armitage has Thorin's 'lion's mane' wig applied; the beard is his own.*

'IT WAS AN INTENSELY COLLABORATIVE PROCESS, BUT THIRTEEN CHARACTERS TOOK A LOT OF DISCUSSING AND, AFTER SIX WEEKS OF DELIBERATIONS, I FINALLY SAID, "WE'RE GOING TO HAVE TO STOP TALKING ABOUT WIGS AND BEARDS AND START MAKING THEM!"'

Peter details some of the different looks: 'Thorin has a lion's mane of flowing hair, a regal look suited to his position as leader; Dwalin's bald, tattooed head reinforces the fact that he is the most warrior-like of the company; Bifur, who has an axe lodged in his head, has a mass of crazy hair that's always matted and tangled because, half the time, he really doesn't know what's going

on; Gloin has the same red hair as his son, Gimli; Nori has a kind of starburst effect inspired by his cheeky, wide-boy character; Dori's hair is an immensely complicated and precise arrangement of plaits reflecting his rather fussy and pernickety personality; Ori, the youngest of the group who probably oughtn't even to be on this adventure, has wispy hair and a pudding-basin hair-cut that was probably given him by one of his brothers using an actual pudding-basin!'

There have been many advances in make-up processes since Peter was working on *The Return of the King*, not least the substitution of silicon prosthetics for the foam latex used previously. 'It is brilliant,' enthuses Peter, 'because it moulds to the skin and moves with the natural movements of the actor's face; and, because it can carry lots of detailing such as all the little wrinkles and veins of human skin, it looks so much more natural and, therefore, realistic.'

The quest for realism is something he feels strongly about: 'Behind the book is an entire mythology created by Tolkien, which gives the story authenticity and demands to be taken seriously. The cast play it like Shakespeare and rightly so. We may be dealing with a fantasy world but it *must* be believable.'

Among Peter's favourite looks created by his department are the sharply contrasting appearance of Thranduil, King of the Wood-elves, with the palest of blond hair and the eccentric Radagast with a bird's nest in his hair and bird-poo on his face.

Peter refuses to be phased by any of the challenges he has faced on *The Hobbit*. 'I've known the people I'm working with for almost twelve years and what we are all trying to do is make the best film possible. Sometimes we're asked to do the *im*possible and I hear myself saying, "Yes, we can do that," and think, "What am I *saying*?" I leave the room without the faintest idea of how we are going to set about it and then just get on and *do* it! Fortunately, the experience I've gathered over those years has meant that I've been able to solve whatever has been thrown at me – *so far!*'

Bifur

'I took one look at the make-up designs,' says William Kircher, 'and thought, "Oh-oh!" Then I thought again and said, "Thank you *very much*!" because it dawned on me: there are thirteen of us and, for the rest of my life, whenever anyone asks, "Which Dwarf were *you*?" I can simply tell them, "I was the one with the axe stuck in my head!"'

ABOVE: *Bifur gets ready to do something unexpected.*
OPPOSITE: *William Kircher. Working in the confines of Bag End, Peter puts Bifur in the frame.*

The decision to have Bifur living with the blade of a hatchet embedded in the front of his skull proved controversial with some Tolkien fans, and led to the launch of an online petition to Peter Jackson to have the offending weapon removed. But, for William, it provided the impetus for an exploration of his screen character.

'It's an Orc axe,' he explains. 'Bifur doesn't remember much about it, but it probably happened in the Dwarf mines during an Orc attack. No one knew how to safely dislodge it, so it was left there. Now he's on his own personal journey: to find the Orc that did this terrible thing to him and pay him back. In the meantime, *any* Orc will do.'

Implausible as it may sound, there are various accounts of real people living with such wounds for many years. However, as William continues, in the case of Bifur the event had a secondary effect: 'He has problems with his memory: he can only speak ancient Dwarvish (which Gandalf alone understands) and, quite a lot of the time, doesn't know where he is. As an actor that gives me a whole lot of things to explore: in any situation, I'll think, "How might Bifur react in a way that's different to the others?" There are times when he has to run and fight and be part of the team, but there are others when he will do something totally unexpected, and that's a joy and a challenge.'

For example, at the feast held in Elrond's chambers at Rivendell, William asked the prop department to make sure that there were some fresh flowers on the table: 'I suddenly thought that it might be quite interesting if, while everyone else is tucking in – well, throwing food around, actually – Bifur (who's a vegetarian) just sat there quietly eating the flowers!'

In the screenplay, Bifur and his cousins are mining folk from the west of Middle-earth: 'We're more rough and ready than the others,' says William, 'we're working class and proud of it. We work hard and we fight hard.'

'HE HAS PROBLEMS WITH HIS MEMORY: HE CAN ONLY
SPEAK ANCIENT DWARVISH (WHICH GANDALF ALONE
UNDERSTANDS) AND, QUITE A LOT OF THE TIME,
DOESN'T KNOW WHERE HE IS.'

And, despite his handicap, Bifur is a fearless fighter. 'If you were going to select three Dwarves to have a scrap with, then you *wouldn't* pick Bifur, Bofur and Bombur! They are *dangerous* – especially Bifur, who is in some sort of parallel universe to the other Dwarves and doesn't know when to stop. When Bifur fights, he just goes nuts!'

William is another Kiwi cast member: 'It's bringing it home,' he says, 'and it is much appreciated.' A graduate of the New Zealand Drama School, he is a veteran of over one hundred theatrical productions as well as numerous appearances on film and television, including a regular role in the Wellington police drama series, *Shark in the Park*.

In 2006, he appeared in the acclaimed movie, *Out of the Blue*, playing Stu Guthrie, the heroic policeman (and winner of the George Cross) shot during the true-life events of the 1990 Aramoana massacre. Starring alongside him was Karl Urban, who played Éomer in *The Lord of the Rings*.

With many recent years of experience as a TV producer and executive, William embraced the opportunity to return to acting in *The Hobbit*. He relishes the role of Bifur, even in moments when the job proved unexpectedly demanding, as with the scene in which the Trolls tie up the Dwarves and put them on a spit to roast. 'That was an interesting experience,' he recalls, 'we were really tied onto a spit and we were up there for about half an hour, going round and round, acting our butts off in extreme conditions. It was quite fun, really, but when we got off we were all pretty queasy as if we'd got a bad case of sea-sickness.'

When the thirteen actors who play Thorin's Company of Dwarves wore their costumes and make-up for the first time, they greeted each other's transformed appearances with a degree of jocularity. 'To start with, there was a lot of hooting and hollering, because we looked so outrageously different. But we then went through this bizarre period of coming to recognize each other with our alternative faces on and now we're all very comfortable in our Dwarf skins and relate to each other completely as our characters. In fact, it now sometimes feels a bit odd when we look at each other *without* our make-up!'

Bofur

'I would have thought myself to be the least likely actor to go into *The Hobbit* and go on that journey and now I'm probably the happiest of everyone!'

James Nesbitt is talking about being cast as Bofur. The Northern Ireland-born actor had not read *The Hobbit* and didn't know much about it, but the casting agency was aware that he had not been considered for many roles in blockbuster productions. 'To tell the truth,' he says, 'I've always been too busy and didn't think it was necessarily the right thing for my career.'

That award-winning career has seen James on stage in everything from Shakespeare via musicals to political dramas; on television, where he was Adam Williams in *Cold Feet*, Tommy Murphy in *Murphy's Law* and, recently, Gabriel Monroe in the medical drama series, *Monroe*; and on film, beginning with his debut in *Hear My Song*. Other significant appearances include the films *Waking Ned*, *Lucky Break*, *Bloody Sunday*, *Five Minutes of Heaven* and *Coriolanus* and his Golden Globe-nominated performance as Tom Jackman and Mr Hyde in the TV drama series, *Jekyll*.

Despite being uncertain about the prospect of a lengthy production on the other side of the world, James gave a videotaped audition: 'I wasn't working at the time,' he recalls, 'so I hadn't shaved and had a bit of a growth around my chin. Maybe I was deliberately, but subconsciously, growing a Dwarf beard! Anyway, I was given a couple of pages to read and, afterwards, I thought to myself, "That went really rather well." And then I wondered, "Do I *want* it to have gone well?"'

It certainly went well enough for James to get a call to go to London to meet with Peter and the producers: 'They were people I immediately thought I wanted to work with and they were very persuasive, in a lovely way. They sold me the notion of the film and of coming down with my family to New Zealand and being a part of the adventure. I was fascinated by the fact that *The Lord of the Rings* – that huge juggernaut of a project that was so influential – was, somehow controlled by this little group of friends in the corner of a place eleven-and-a-half thousand miles away. I went into that meeting thinking, "I will not be doing *The Hobbit*!" I walked out of the meeting thinking, "I've *got* to do *The Hobbit*!"

James' character, Bofur, is accompanied by his several times larger-than-life brother, Bombur, and his cousin, Bifur, who is somewhat challenged on account of the axe embedded in his skull. Describing the trio, James says: 'We're quite rough, simple folk, my clan. And we are Irish. Well, *I* am; Stephen and William are doing Irish accents – *very good* Irish accents.'

James' natural accent is very much a part of his personality as an actor. 'Unless the character I am playing absolutely has to be from somewhere else, it has always been important for me to use my own accent. There was a time when Northern Ireland was viewed by the rest of the world simply in terms of the conflicts there, but I wanted to use the accent without any political baggage, simply as a place where someone comes from.'

To James' great delight, the filmmakers accepted that he would play Bofur in a Northern Irish accent. 'I think that Peter and the others were looking to include bits of me in the character, so it was important not only that I should remain Irish, but that the character should have a level of charm and optimism. As Bofur develops, I think you'll see his serious side and his fierceness, but essentially he is an optimistic Dwarf, someone who is a bit of a joker and who can lighten the mood.'

James feels that Bofur has a particular affinity with Mr Baggins. 'I think he sees in Bilbo someone who is isolated among the Company of Dwarves just as he is initially rather isolated. He doesn't have much communication with the other, classier Dwarves or with his own folk, since Bifur only ever speaks in old Dwarvish and Bombur is too busy eating to talk much at all. Also Bofur sees and respects something noble and courageous in Bilbo's character.'

In contrast to his initial reservations about the project, James Nesbitt now talks about it in terms of pure joy: 'It's like grown-ups playing, really. If you see young boys between, say, five and seven: all they do is run around and play. And that's basically what we've been doing – the big difference is we're getting paid to have fun!'

OPPOSITE: *Bofur enjoys himself in Bag End.* BELOW: *Bofur will need all his cheerful optimism when things get difficult in scene 129.*

STEPHEN HUNTER

Bombur

With his almost spherical body shape and fiery red loop of beard, Bombur is possibly the most distinctive of the Dwarves. Adding to his already unusual appearance are several bright turquoise hairgrips attached to his beard and hair. The reason? Stephen Hunter, who plays him, is on his lunch break in *The Hobbit* catering marquee. 'I use these,' he explains, 'in an attempt to keep my whiskers out of my food and vice versa. The trouble is, I'm not always successful!'

Food is a frequent topic of conversation with Stephen, especially when he is talking about Bombur: 'The distinguishing feature of my character is that he is eating all the time. Bombur loves food; he's a real foodie. He's got everything he needs – all the herbs, a couple of ladles and his pot – and he's ready to cook.'

Bombur's fondness for cooking and eating inevitably has an effect: 'Let's not beat about the bush,' says Stephen, 'Bombur is a fat Dwarf. He's the biggest of them all. But big guys seem to do pretty well with the ladies because we've decided that he has a lot of children – *twelve* at the last count! There's not a lot of Dwarf women around so I guess you have to make hay while the sun shines, so to speak.'

As described by Tolkien, Bombur is clumsy and accident-prone and has to endure a variety of undignified mishaps. 'It would have been simple,' says Stephen, 'to have just made him the guy who likes to eat a lot and is a bit hopeless. I wanted to create something more for Bombur, because I love the fact that he's a massive unit who is completely comfortable with who he is. He's up for anything – biding his time, chipping away, doing his job – and there's still a lot that's going to happen to him about which he has really no idea. The same, of course, could be said for me as an actor.'

One of the cast's Kiwi contingent, Stephen was born and bred a Wellingtonian and began his acting career on New Zealand television before moving to Australia where he became known for playing the character, Sharpie, in the award-winning drama series, *Love My Way*. He subsequently appeared in the medical drama, *All Saints*, and displayed his comedic talents on the satirical *Review with Myles Barlow*.

Stephen was a keen fan of *The Lord of the Rings*: 'I'd read all the books about the trilogy, seen the extended DVDs with all the behind-the-scenes footage. I felt that I really wanted to be part of that world and had earmarked *The Hobbit* as a project with which I wanted to be involved.'

Stephen's agent in New Zealand put him forward to the casting directors and he received a call to attend an audition in Auckland. 'I could have auditioned remotely from Sydney but decided it was better to be there in person. I did a lot of preparation work on the script, grew a shaggy beard, let my hair grow out, wore an old ripped-up shirt and did a really good audition. I walked out thinking, "I reckon I'll get something here." Three months later, having heard nothing, I was on a visit to Wellington and talking with friends about how great it would be if I got a part in the film and was working there. The very next morning – *bang!* – I got a phone call to say I'd been offered the role of Bombur.'

Bombur is taking part in the Quest with his brother Bofur and his cousin Bifur. 'We are scrappers!' says Stephen. 'We don't share the royal lineage of some of the others. We're pretty much the hackers of the Dwarf world. Rough and ready. For us, the Quest is about kicking some Orc butt, taking the mountain, killing the dragon and getting a bit of gold. Scrappers and hackers, that's what we three are!'

With thirteen Dwarves to individually characterize, the question was how would Bombur be presented? 'I was asked if I was happy to not have so many lines but, instead, to concentrate on the physical aspects of the character. The actor's first instinct is always, "How many lines do I get to say?" But that's not really an indicator of how your character is going to be seen and remembered, so I really embraced the physicality of the role.'

For Stephen this meant having to learn to cope with the character's shape and size. He has a full prosthetic make-up that covers all his own face apart from the eyes and wears a huge body suit under his costume. 'It was,' he says, 'a bit uncomfortable to start with, but as it is made of foam it's bulky rather than heavy or uncomfortable – although it does certainly get hot in there.'

To keep the body temperature down, Stephen consumes a lot of drinks to keep hydrated and wears a cool-vest piped through with iced water. Nevertheless, there are times when it can feel as if he is acting in a portable sauna. 'Everybody told me: "You'll lose so much weight", but I haven't because they give you such good lunches here and I just can't keep away from them; so rather than losing weight I have actually been putting it on!'

While he's having lunch, Stephen has shed various bits of Bombur's bulky anatomy. He explains: 'I'm careful not to put on all of the parts of the costume until I'm ready to actually shoot a scene. In fact one day I walked on set and had forgotten to put my stomach on and nobody even seemed to notice – which was a bit disturbing!'

OPPOSITE: *Bombur, the biggest Dwarf of them all.* TOP TO BOTTOM: *Bombur enjoys some Elven hospitality. Doing what he loves best. Stephen Hunter.*

BERT, TOM & WILLIAM

The Trollshaw Trio

Travelling to Rivendell in *The Fellowship of the Ring* film, Frodo and his companions make camp in the shadow of a trio of petrified trolls. These gigantic characters were turned to stone, many years earlier, following an encounter with Bilbo and the Dwarves that Tolkien describes in *The Hobbit* and which Peter Jackson is now depicting on film.

The Trolls – named Bert, Tom and William – are digitally animated using reference footage gathered through the motion-capture (mocap) process. A live-action camera films – or captures – actors performing the characters' movements while wearing suits and face masks covered with tracking dots. These markers are subsequently used by the digital artists in creating the creatures to be seen on screen. Famously pioneered with Gollum in *The Lord of the Rings*, mocap enables digital characters, however fantastical, to have lifelike actions and express identifiably human emotions.

Three members of the Dwarf cast supplied the mocap footage for the Trolls: Mark Hadlow plays Bert and Peter Hambleton, William, while, confusingly, William Kircher was cast, not as his namesake, but as Tom.

'It was really disconcerting,' says Peter, 'playing William, while William was playing someone else! Compared with his mates, my Troll has got the least developed sense of humour. I think he sees himself as the leader of the group although the other two would probably beg to differ.'

'We had such fun,' recalls Mark. 'Peter Jackson was in extraordinarily playful mood and it was a

ABOVE RIGHT: *Mark Hadlow, William Kircher & Peter Hambleton rehearse their moves in the mo-cap studio.* RIGHT: *Meanwhile, on the actual Trollshaw Forest set, Peter acts as a Troll for the camera, while the 'real thing' looks down from its pole. This will give the Dwarf actors the correct eyeline when performing against the Trolls.*

fascinating experience because we were able to see on screen what was being filmed. It was really rather hard to act out the movements without constantly collapsing with laughter at how we looked.'

'Although the Trolls are not quite the Middle-earth equivalent of the Three Stooges,' says William, 'there is a good deal of slapstick comedy involved in their scenes: fun stuff that we'd invent on the day, working closely with Peter Jackson in the very contained and focused environment of the mocap studio.'

Peter Hambleton was similarly excited by the process: 'It is such an astonishing concept: that the brilliantly clever Digital people will work their artistry and make these creatures come to life but that – inside them – will be our performances.'

The trio had done preparatory work with Movement

Coach, Terry Notary, and someone who was well experienced in the challenges of mocap acting, Andy Serkis. 'The first thing Andy suggested,' remembers William, 'was that we consider what injuries these characters might have had in the past. What do they bring with them that will affect how they move? I put weights on an arm and on a leg so that I could act as if those limbs were dead. This gave me a very physical way of playing the character that looked really good, although I almost regretted having the idea because it was such incredibly hard work.'

Since the Dwarves are captured in a fight with the Trolls, William, Mark and Peter had the uncanny experience of filming these scenes twice. 'When I was playing William the Troll during the fight,' says Peter, 'I was simulating the excruciating pain of having my lower legs chopped at by a Dwarf and then, when playing Gloin, I was imagining that I was attacking William with my axe. I feel that having a fight with myself could turn out to be the pinnacle of my acting career!'

On the nature of Trolls in general, Mark says: 'Trolls are huge, horrible creatures, that will eat just about anything or anybody. They're not especially partial to Dwarves, because there's not that much meat on them, but if there's nothing else about they will spit-roast a few or use them to make a nice Dwarf hotpot.' Surprisingly, Mark found some affinity between the two characters he plays: 'Bert the Troll,' he explains, 'is quite similar to Dori the Dwarf, in that they both enjoy their food and love cooking. The difference is that Bert will fry up everything: shoes, bits of nails and bones, and pretty much anything you can chew or crunch!'

Grotesque though the Trolls are, all three actors developed an affection for their monstrous alter egos, and Peter is hoping that William, Bert and Tom may manage to find a career after *The Hobbit*: 'Although we are eventually turned into stone, I am sure there must be some way of breaking the spell. If so, then I can really see a series of spin-off movies featuring the further adventures of the Trolls in Middle-earth.'

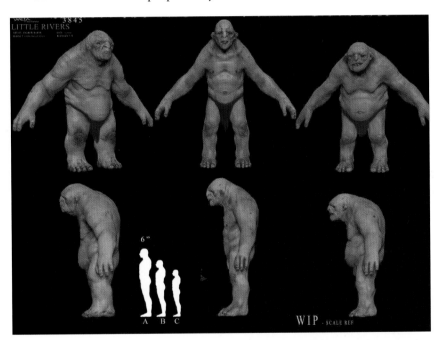

Radagast: The Wizard Who Talks to the Animals

'Radagast is a wizard,' says Sylvester McCoy, 'and so, obviously, I have a beard and a lot of hair with, I have to say, quite a lot of bird poo in it. I've also got a snaggled tooth and, of course, a nose. *Everybody* on this film has a nose, but they've given me a bent version of my *own* nose! I can't help feeling that I could have saved them money by just going out on to the street and picking a fight with somebody: then I shouldn't need make-up and wouldn't have to get up quite so early in the mornings!'

Sylvester is talking about his character in *The Hobbit* at the end of a busy day on set where his imagination has had to work overtime. 'I do a lot of my acting in front of green-screen so that, later on, they can add in digital backgrounds and all Radagast's animal friends. This means I spend most of my time talking to invisible creatures! I feel like Bob Hoskins in *Who Framed Roger Rabbit*. He told me he nearly went mad doing that film, so I'm doing my level best to keep sane.'

In an extensive stage and television career, Sylvester is internationally known as the seventh incarnation of the time-travelling Doctor in the iconic BBC SF drama, *Doctor Who*. As he recalls, he was also very nearly Bilbo Baggins in *The Lord of the Rings*: 'It got down to a choice between Ian Holm and myself for the part and, basically, if Ian had got another job that week I would have been Bilbo.'

The invitation to join the cast of *The Hobbit* came when Sylvester was on a tour of New Zealand with the Royal Shakespeare Company's 2008 production of *King Lear,* in which he played the Fool to Ian McKellen's Lear: 'I had a distant memory of reading *The Hobbit* sometime back in the Sixties – slightly stoned, I imagine – so I rushed out to get the book and looked all through it for Radagast, thinking, "So, where *is* he?" Then

ABOVE: *Sylvester rehearses his lines with Ian McKellen, while a crew member checks the script.* RIGHT: *Radagast the Wizard, with one of his healing potions.*

they explained how the character had been left out of *The Lord of the Rings* and how he would be developed. What's more, they assured me that they were going to write me a bigger part than if I'd played Bilbo in *Rings*!'

The fact that Radagast is only a shadowy character in the Tolkien mythology with just one brief mention in *The Hobbit*, where Beorn refers to him as 'not a bad fellow as wizards go', has provided the screenwriters and Sylvester with a degree of freedom in developing the role. 'I see him as being very otherworldly with, as Tolkien depicts him, an empathy and kinship with nature, rather like a Middle-earth version of St Francis of Assisi. Although he is somewhat vague and forgetful, he eventually emerges as a kind of bumbling hero.'

Of Radagast's extraordinary home in Rhosgobel, Sylvester says: 'What happened was that a tree decided to grow up through his house and, being Radagast, he said, "Well, if you want to grow, you can grow, and you can live with me and I'll live with you." And so, between them, they created this wonderful house.'

For Sylvester, the chance to work with Peter Jackson and his associates is a much-welcomed opportunity: 'One of the blessings of the place is that it is totally unlike any studio in Hollywood or London. The atmosphere is utterly different: much less pressure, much more relaxed. Everyone works incredibly hard but they do it with such spirit that you hardly notice the hard work – until you wake up the next morning and can barely move!'

Sylvester has a few aches and pains from a minor mishap while filming a scene involving Radagast's idiosyncratic way of getting around Middle-earth – a sled pulled by enormous rabbits. 'I know what the rabbits look like and I love the fact that they all have individual characteristics, but when I'm filming, of course, I can't *see* them – well, only in my mind. Anyway, I was galloping along with wind machines blowing me and my costume all over the place and I flew right off the sled. That's the trouble with rabbits – they just don't have very good road sense!'

OPPOSITE: *Radagast stands outside his home, Rhosgobel, one of the massive sets that began life as conceptual drawings by John Howe and Alan Lee.* TOP: *Sylvester prepares for Radagast's next scene as 1st AD, Second Unit, Liz Tan prepares the shot.* ABOVE: *Radagast about to discover something nasty in Mirkwood.*

Where did the Rabbits Come From?

Ask anyone involved in the production of *The Hobbit* who was responsible for Radagast driving a sled pulled by rabbits and the finger points to one man… 'We wanted him to be an engaging, character,' says Philippa Boyens, 'but the sled? *That* was Pete's idea!'

Confessing to having dreamt up this embellishment, Peter Jackson says: 'We were always intrigued by what Tolkien wrote about Radagast, although there's not a lot about him in the books beyond the fact that he seems to have had a very real affinity with birds and animals. In expanding on that idea it seemed obvious to give him a mode of transport that was unique – like a bunny-rabbit sled.' With a laugh he adds: 'We took a lot of things from Tolkien's appendices to *The Lord of the Rings*, but I admit that wasn't one of them!'

Top: *Peter reads the script to find out what happens next between Gandalf and Radagast.* Above: *Peter shares a joke with Ian McKellen while Sylvester looks for rabbits.*

134

Clothes Lines

ANN MASKREY ON DRESSING RADAGAST

'I love Radagast's costume because it encompasses almost every skill in our workshop: those responsible for textiles, dying, printing and embroidery. Every craft from top to toe: the milliner to the boot-maker.

'I wanted to create the look of an eccentric person from the woodlands using as many different textures as possible in the design.

'Under everything, Radagast has a really scruffy pair of long johns that we made to be nice and baggy in the crotch. Over these, he wears several layers of clothing, all of which look old and worn, including two waistcoats, the outer one made in a fabric with a metallic thread that we had woven in Britain. Over this are two layers of dyed chiffon embroidered with seventeenth-century chain stitch in a pattern of my own featuring trees, rabbits and butterflies. The buttons are mismatched and it's meant to be done up wrongly in a mad way – rather like I do up my cardigan in the morning when I'm in a rush!

'Finally, he has a top layer of a ragged velvet coat with the pile worn away, a furry wizard hat without a point, but with what look like rabbitty ears, and, because Peter wanted him to have an asymmetrical look, odd shoes: one velvet brocade slipper and a leather, curly toed boot.'

CLOCKWISE FROM ABOVE: *Ann Maskrey's costume designs of Radagast, in a hurry and with one of his team of rabbits. Ann in the Wardrobe workroom surrounded by her designs, embroidery and sample fabrics.*

Making Faces in Middle-earth

'The first time you wear a prosthetic nose, it is a bit like wearing a new shoe: to start with, it feels a bit tight and weird, but by the end of the day you hardly notice.'

Prosthetics Supervisor, Tami Lane, is talking about an experience that the majority of cast members on *The Hobbit* have been through in getting into their characters.

'Our noses,' says Tami, 'are very light and flexible so it is not long before the actors are scarcely aware of them – unless, of course, they can see the *end* of their nose, in which case it may take a bit longer!'

Tami is American but is no stranger to Peter Jackson's Wellington-based studio: like many others, she worked on *The Lord of the Rings* and now has New Zealand citizenship.

The most significant change between filming *Rings* and *The Hobbit* is the increased number of characters requiring prosthetic make-up. Gimli was the only major Dwarf in the trilogy; now there are thirteen, plus their various doubles.

There are individual make-up designs for each of the Dwarves, ranging from simply a nose for Kili, via foreheads, and noses to an entire face prosthetic for Bombur.

During the ten years since Gimli battled his way from Moria to the Black Gates, prosthetic make-up has made great advances, as Tami explains: 'Previously, we used

LEFT: *Tami Lane concentrates on transforming an extra into one of the Orcs.* ABOVE: *The Orc smiles for the camera while his finished prosthetic receives its final touches on-set, ready to film in HD.*

standard industry materials, foam latex and gelatine, but advances with camera technology have required comparable improvements in the make-up department. Now, everything from facial prosthetics for the Dwarves to hobbit feet are made from a material called encapsulated silicon – which is quicker and easier to apply and more realistic: foam latex looked flat, but silicon has all the texture of a real skin surface.'

The downside is that it is more expensive and less hardwearing: 'When a prosthetic piece is applied to an actor's face, the edges can be blended away onto the skin so that there are no telltale joins, but there is no way of saving the piece when the make-up is removed at the end of the day's shooting. With foam latex, prosthetics could be used for three shoots, now it's a case of fresh on every day.'

The tight pre-production schedule on *The Hobbit* meant that the make-up department didn't have sufficient time to stockpile adequate supplies. 'We get our new prosthetics each day,' says Tami, 'and because most of the actors wear a forehead, eyebrows have to be added to each silicon piece. Hand-punched – one hair at a time – with a needle, this takes up to two hours for each character and keeps us busy while filming is going on. We get in at four o'clock in the morning, hit the road running and keep going until, sometimes, nine at night.'

The original prosthetic make-up designs began at Weta Workshop with ideas overlaid by computer onto photographs of life-casts taken of the actors' heads. Next, clay models were made so that Peter Jackson and his colleagues could select the various individual looks they wanted. Once the designs had been refined, moulds were made and from these the silicon face-parts can be repeatedly manufactured.

'For a while,' recalls Tami, 'it was an on-going project, because prosthetics only seen on the head cast of an actor tend to look different when they are on a living person who is moving and talking. Bofur took a while to find his final appearance: to start with he had an enormous nose and a heavy brow and was a bit of an angry Dwarf! The

problem was that the prosthetic was overpowering actor James Nesbitt's face, whereas what we have now is a Dwarf version of Jimmy.'

The average time for a Dwarf make-up application is around an hour-and-a-quarter: Kili gets off lightly with just half-an-hour, while the heavyweight Bombur has to endure two hours in the chair.

Once the prosthetics are applied, they are painted with skin tone, freckles and, for the older Dwarves, liver spots – applied using stencils so that they are always in the same place.

'Each Dwarf has his own colour,' explains Tami. 'For example, Nori leads a more rugged, outdoor life and so has a sun-kissed skin tone; whereas Dori, who prefers the comforts of his home rather than being outside, has a skin-tone that is much lighter.'

Multiply the number of Dwarves by whatever doubles are required for a sequence and it takes on the feel of a production line.

'WE GET IN AT FOUR O'CLOCK
IN THE MORNING, HIT THE
ROAD RUNNING AND KEEP
GOING UNTIL, SOMETIMES,
NINE AT NIGHT.'

On the part of the actors, prosthetic make-up
(even in its newer, lighter form) requires a fair
amount of stamina: 'Sometimes the actors get very
hot under the lights on set and sweat so heavily
that it builds up under the silicon make-up pieces.
That's when we have to – as we call it – "milk"
our actors! I am constantly impressed, but not surprised, at how well they cope with having what is
really a weird kind of facial every single day!'

RIGHT: *Tami and her assistant ensure that Cate
Blanchett's hair and make-up are fit for the Lady
Galadriel.*

139

CLOCKWISE FROM TOP: *Surrounded by the tools of his trade, and reference photos, a make-up artist goes to work on an Orc. Graham McTavish enjoys some personal grooming that will turn him into Dwalin. Lunch is served for the Goblins!*

LEFT: *One of the new-look hobbit feet, which is now a knee-length silicon boot that can be easily pulled on, instead of the latex shoe that had to be painstakingly glued on and detached in* The Lord of the Rings. BELOW: *A hobbit extra tries not to giggle as his silicon feet are pulled on.*

BELOW: *Three members of the 'on-set' Make-up team, who work on location, busy themselves adding hair to hobbit feet during a break in production.*

Arming the Dwarves

Thirteen, some say, is an unlucky number and that could well be the case for any creature falling foul of Thorin's Company of Dwarves and their serious array of weapons. 'The Dwarves go through multiple changes of armaments during the course of the two films,' says Weta Workshop's Richard Taylor. 'They lose and gain various weapons, but when we meet them at Bag End on the first stage of the journey they carry a motley collection of fairly worn-in bits of weaponry that they've had for a long time and which, if they were ever grand, are far from being so now.'

ABOVE: *The Dwarves work as a team to fight their enemies, ensuring that they are protected from all sides.*
RIGHT: *Dori shows off his bolas.*

'What I love about the Dwarf fighting style,' says Richard Armitage, 'is that it's all about damage and power. There's not a huge amount of finesse involved. It's all about the swing and, in a way, having a heavy weapon is very useful because it's about getting your body behind the weapon and allowing the weight of the weapon to do the damage.'

Richard Taylor agrees: 'Everything is stocky, broad and heavy because Dwarves are incredibly powerful and able to swing enormous chunks of metal around that would totally exhaust a human.'

Except, of course, that the Dwarves using these particular weapons are actors – *and human*! Richard, as Thorin, uses the Elven sword, Orcrist (translated from Elvish as 'Goblin Cleaver'), which he finds among the plunder of the Trolls and has a handle made from a dragon's tooth: 'It's really heavy and really long (in fact, it's almost as big as me) and in order to be able to wield it in a rapid series of figure-of-eight movements,

'WHAT I LOVE ABOUT THE DWARF FIGHTING STYLE,' SAYS RICHARD ARMITAGE, 'IS THAT IT'S ALL ABOUT DAMAGE AND POWER.'

I've really had to do some serious work on both my grip and on building up my forearm strength.'

As for Graham McTavish, one of the most seriously fit members of the cast, he has to manage Dwalin's war-hammer: 'It is huge and heavy and you really think there's no way to make it look convincing. I remember the first time I swung the hammer everybody standing off camera was flinching because they thought I was going to let go! As *if*… I'd been well trained by the sword master and in no time I was zooming about – *Boom-boom-boom-boom-boom!* – taking on five Goblins at once.'

Speaking of the Company as a whole, Graham says: 'We've got a ridiculous array of weaponry between us, although some have more than others. Fili, for example, has practically everything, including the kitchen sink, attached to his body!'

Dean O'Gorman confirms that his character is a one-Dwarf walking arsenal: 'He's like a hedgehog. He's bristling with all these armaments, including two swords, a couple of daggers and, at the beginning of the journey, ankle-axes as well. Since Fili is always up for a fight – especially if there are any Orcs involved – he's always got his weapons at the ready.'

Aidan Turner plays Fili's brother, Kili: 'Essentially, he's another fighter and an adept archer. A young guy, Kili is always ready to smash a few heads and, as well as being able to handle swords and axes, he is a skilful bowman.'

Ken Stott, who plays Balin, says: 'My character has a short sword, that is, in a sense, his badge of office as Thorin's counsellor, but a number of the actors have invented all kinds of

interesting methods of warfare: some fun but *all* totally lethal!'

Weta Workshop did, indeed, involve cast members in the weapon design process, as John Callen, playing Oin, explains: 'Some of the Dwarves have axes, others huge hammers – almost like battering rams. Some only use swords: a two-handed sword, perhaps, or a sword in each hand. All this was discussed with the individual actors and developed to a point where we could settle who's having what weapons and then start working out how to use them. Oin has ended up with a very large staff – over two meters long – which he has to wield. He can also use it to lean on when he needs a rest, but basically it's a very pointy stick and if you're something bigger than a Dwarf (such as a Troll) that's the one thing you don't want to have jabbed in your eye or any other

sensitive parts of your anatomy! It's really useful but just in case it gets damaged or broken, Oin has a couple of little knives tucked away in the back of his belt.'

For Jed Brophy the chance to choose weapons provided an opportunity to reflect something of his character's background. 'Because Nori has led a wanderer's life, I decided that he would have weapons that he'd found or adapted rather than inherited from his ancestors. So his main weapon is made out of an old mining tool that he picked up on his travels. However, not surprisingly since he's a bit of a backstabber, he also loves daggers.'

The consultation process resulted in Dwalin acquiring – in addition to his hammer (*and* two axes and a knife) – another interesting item of warmongery, as Graham reveals: 'I have a pair of knuckle-dusters. I mentioned that I saw Dwalin as the kind of guy whose hands are as much of a weapon as his hammer. So if he ever finds himself with no weapons, he still has his hands. That led to a discussion about the possibility of armoured gauntlets and how it would be good to have something that was articulated. Then Richard Taylor, being the genius that he is, came up with spring-loaded knuckle-dusters that will probably be responsible for some serious Orc damage.'

For Richard Armitage the collaboration with Weta Workshop's designers resulted in a unique creation. Thorin earned his name 'Oakenshield' many years before the events described in *The Hobbit*. At the climactic battle of the wars between the Dwarves and the Orcs, Thorin had led a Dwarf army into the valley below the eastern gate of Moria. During the fray, Thorin's shield was broken and he chopped a branch from an oak tree with which to defend himself.

'Thorin already had a substantial sword,' says Richard, 'clearly the noble weapon of a king, and on the journey he acquires the Elf-blade, Orcrist. Then I came up with an idea that I didn't really think would go anywhere, but that Peter Jackson quite liked. I thought that maybe Thorin had preserved the branch he'd used as a weapon at the Battle of Azanulbizar. With age it had taken on the consistency and strength of iron and he had created a sort of gauntlet from it. With two metal hooks on the back, he had turned it into a multi-purpose weapon that can be used either to punch or as a shield, much as he would have done with the original branch. It may – or may not – ever make it into a battle

LEFT TO RIGHT: *A Dwarven arsenal: Thorin's Elven sword, Orcrist; Nori's fleshing knife; Kili's sword; Ori's slingshot; Gloin's axe; Balin's sword; Dori's bolas; Bifur's boar-spear; Nori's staff; Fili's warhammer; Bofur's mattock; one of Dwalin's knuckle-dusters, and his pair of axes, Grasper and Keeper.*

sequence, but I like having it and I also like the fact that this original weapon is now known as the "Oakenshield".'

For the character of Gloin, the choice of weapon was easily agreed as Peter Hambleton explains: 'I have a small knife and a throwing axe, but most of the time Gloin carries the same big axe as was brandished by Gimli in *The Lord of the Rings* trilogy. At the time when *The Hobbit* is set, it is still Gloin's axe but, sixty years later, it will be inherited by his son.'

At least one of the Dwarves would quite like to exchange his weapon for a more manageable alternative. 'Bofur is a great fighter,' says James Nesbitt, 'and since he's quite a rough and dirty scrapper, his weaponry is quite crude. Whereas other Dwarves take great pride in the majesty and the grandeur of their swords, Bofur just has a mattock with a horrible point to it and a very thick head, both of which would do a lot of harm. But it's a nightmare! It's so heavy it gave me tendonitis and stopped me playing golf for three months. So I'd trade it in like a shot!'

'IT'S ALL ABOUT THE SWING AND, IN A WAY, HAVING A HEAVY WEAPON IS VERY USEFUL BECAUSE IT'S ABOUT GETTING YOUR BODY BEHIND THE WEAPON AND ALLOWING THE WEIGHT OF THE WEAPON TO DO THE DAMAGE.'

There are some unusual weapons among the company, such as Bifur's boar-spear, which can be used by driving the heel into the earth, holding it at an angle and allowing the charging enemy to impale itself. 'The look of it is incredible,' says William Kircher, 'it's got a spike at one end, but it's also an axe. It's really very different – rather like Bifur himself – and it gives me a silhouette that is like nobody else's. I love it!'

Dori wields the even more exotic bolas: 'They are three big metal balls on the end of the chain,' Mark Hadlow explains, 'which I whirl around my head. I also have a small strike sword and I can use both weapons at the same time. Dori looks pretty menacing when he gets mad and starts swinging that bolas.'

It might be tempting to under-rate the slingshot used by Dori's younger brother, Ori, but probably unwise. 'It might look nothing,' says Adam Brown, 'especially when compared with those big swords used by Kili and Fili, but it is *deadly*!'

Bombur's combination of armaments is probably the most unlikely. As a foodaholic who has all his cooking utensils permanently to hand, he can lay about him with a particularly large ladle. He has also found a sinister use for his lengthy hairpiece. 'It's a distinctive look,' says Stephen Hunter, of Bombur's curious scarf-like interweaving of hair and beard. 'He's very proud of it and it can serve for many things, like collecting food that he can't reach off the table, but it's also handy as a weapon. "Strangler", I call it, because it's very useful for disposing of the odd little Goblin!'

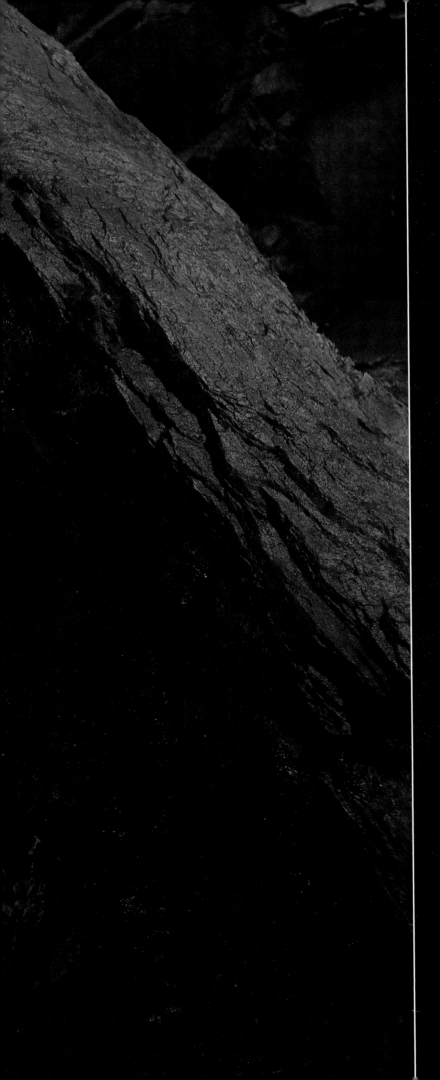

Foe-hammer & Sting

Two significant blades, familiar to audiences of *The Lord of the Rings*, make their first appearance in *The Hobbit*. Among the Elven weapons discovered among the Troll's treasure horde is the sword, Glamdring (or 'Foe-hammer'), which Gandalf takes and uses in the War of the Ring, and the small knife that provides Mr Baggins with a hobbit-sized sword. After one significant encounter with the creatures of Middle-earth Bilbo will name it Sting, and it will be later engraved by smiths with an Elvish inscription. Long after his adventures 'there and back again', Bilbo will pass the blade on to Frodo when he embarks on his journey to take the Ring to Rivendell.

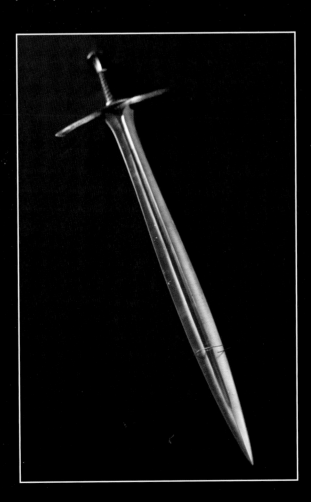

LEFT: *Bilbo prepares to use his new sword.* ABOVE: *The Elven blade, Glamdring, that will become Gandalf's sword during* The Hobbit *and* The Lord of the Rings.

High Definition, High Expectations

I f you hear mention of 'The All-seeing Eye of Evil' on *The Hobbit* sets, it is not – as you might think – a reference to the Dark Lord Sauron, but a comment on the film's High Definition digital filming process.

Instead of reels of film, the images go directly onto two digital memory cards, one each for the twin eyes of the 3D cameras. This enables the capture of 2–3 terabytes a day that is then downloaded and backed up, after which the memory card is wiped and re-used. This allows for a great deal more footage to be shot than would be possible using conventional film stock. Indeed, in the first 100 days on *The Hobbit*, the footage downloaded had already exceeded the entire footage shot on *The Lord of the Rings*.

Many of the anxieties that previously plagued filmmakers are gone for ever: no more worrying about whether or not you managed to get the shot that was wanted; or whether the film was loaded and unloaded without being ruined by light getting in; or whether the 'gate' that guides the film as it runs behind the camera lens was free from hairs and fluff that might show up on film. Also it is possible to film for much longer periods because there is no need to break off while the camera is being reloaded; and with no negative to be developed and printed, there is no longer a 24-hour delay before the shot footage can be viewed and checked.

However, the challenge that comes with this sophistication is that High Definition (or HD) shoots at 48 frames per second, twice the speed of film, which shows everything with the sharpest clarity. 'For the set-decorators it is wonderful,' says Art Department Manager, Chris Hennah. 'All the exquisite props – pottery, hand-blown glass, carved wood – all the delicate and detailed

BELOW: *'Here's looking at you!' Peter and Andrew Lesnie with one of the 3D cameras.* RIGHT: *Bilbo stands on the bridge leading to the* Green Dragon Inn, *with The Mill in the background.*

dressing created for the sets can be seen in all their beauty instead of being out of focus somewhere in the background of a shot.'

But if the new process shows such things to advantage there is the disadvantage of its tendency to reveal things that the filmmakers would rather *not* be seen.

'Filming in HD,' says Jamie Wilson, Weta Workshop Production Manager, 'means that you have to be extra vigilant because there's no way of hiding any blemishes or imperfections. It's not that it sees anything *more*, it is merely that, being in HD, it is less forgiving and every seam, join or chip will be seen for ever in glorious colour high-definition.'

There's also a very specific requirement relating to HD when it comes to one of Weta's

responsibilities, armoury. 'One of the things which HD reveals,' says Jamie 'is if a sword doesn't have a really sharp edge to it. For safety reasons, weapons usually have the edge rounded off, but the fact that it has no cut or thrust to it will clearly be revealed on screen. So we use one of the safety blades for as long as we can, but when it comes to the moment where it is going to be seen in anything approaching close-up, we have to switch it for one that has got a genuinely sharp edge to the blade.'

The Costume Department also have to cope with the potential perils of HD. Ann Maskrey (it is she who dubbed HD the All-seeing Eye of Evil) says: 'There are some fabrics that you wouldn't bat an eyelid about using if you are filming in thirty-five millimetre but which, with HD, we really cannot use. There was a silk brocade material that we were considering for the waistcoat worn by Bilbo at Bag End. We had already looked at several different fabrics that just weren't interesting enough, when we found one that we all thought was absolutely lovely: it was woven with a leaf design and looked perfect. However, seen through the evil eye of the HD camera, that leaf design reflected the light in the weirdest way and came shouting out at you from the screen, as if to say, "Look at me, look at me!" I immediately knew I had to resume my search.'

'IN THE OLD DAYS WE USED TO GET AWAY WITH ALL KINDS OF TRICKS, BUT NOW WE HAVE TO BE MUCH MORE CAREFUL.'

Similar problems affect the Make-up and Hair Department. 'Occasionally,' says Prosthetics Supervisor, Tami Lane, 'we run into difficulties with disguising the edges of the prosthetic make-up we put on the actors. In the old days we used to get away with all kinds of tricks, but now we have to be much more careful. The fact is, in real life, you can be two feet away from an actor in make-up and not notice where a false nose is fixed onto a human face, but photograph it with an HD camera and you see it at once.'

Make-up and Hair Designer, Peter King, takes HD in his stride. The gauze that forms the base of a wig is known as wig lace and it can sometimes be a telltale giveaway if the line where a wig is attached to an actor's forehead is visible on a camera close-up. Peter prides himself on invariably passing what he calls 'the lace test' – even under the relentless scrutiny of the HD camera – but admits to other unexpected difficulties. 'We were using some special make-up,' he recalls, 'that was supposed to give the Dwarves' skin the appearance of being a bit grubby. It contained little bits of black rubber meant to look like specks of dirt, but under the HD camera they looked, at best, like a bad case of blackheads and, at worst, as if they'd got holes all over their faces!'

LEFT TO RIGHT: *The cameras will capture every detail and show them in breathtaking 3D. Work in the mo-cap studio is recorded digitally and reviewed in real-time using CG models. The Art Department delighted in filling Radagast's home of Rhosgobel with a chaotic variety of props, all of which are created to the highest level of detail, ready to be seen in HD.*

Entering the Third Dimension

'I thought it would be exciting to step into Middle-earth in the third dimension.' Peter Jackson is preparing to shoot another scene for *The Hobbit* using 3D cameras.

Peter has always been a fan of 3D and he has frequently used filming techniques that create images with what he calls 'dimensionality'. As he explains: 'I like wide-angle lenses, I like depth, I like composing shots that have a foreground, a middle and a background and I like moving the camera around because it gives dimensionality – a sense of movement within the frame, almost as if you were taking a 2D image and giving it 3D life.'

'I AM REALLY PLEASED THAT WE ARE NOW FILMING *The Hobbit* IN 3D BUT, AS A FILMMAKER, YOU MUST NEVER FORGET THAT WHILE 3D MIGHT MAKE A GOOD MOVIE BETTER, IT'S NEVER GOING TO MAKE A BAD MOVIE GOOD!'

If the technology had been readily available, Peter Jackson would have been shooting 3D before now: 'When we were filming *The Lord of the Rings* I was taking 3D stills and if I could have shot *Rings* in 3D, I'd have done so at the drop of a hat. We nearly shot *King Kong* in 3D. At the time, we met with James Cameron and looked at the equipment he was planning to use to film *Avatar*, but we were just a month away from shooting *Kong* and felt that the technical complexities were just too great for us to master in the time, so we came close – but not close enough. I am really pleased that we are now filming *The Hobbit* in 3D but, as a filmmaker, you must never forget that while 3D might make a good movie better, it's never going to make a bad movie good!'

Peter has to go off to watch a rehearsal of the next scene, and Andrew Lesnie, cinematographer on *The Hobbit* (and, earlier, *The Lord of the Rings*, for which he won an Oscar), takes me off to discover more about the 3D process.

'This is the man,' says Andrew, introducing me to Sean Kelly, the film's Lead Stereographer, 'who can give you an idiot's guide to filming in 3D.'

To be fair, that's exactly what I asked for and, fortunately, Sean is used to de-mystifying a highly technical process without making the listener feel too stupid. 'Instead of one camera,' he explains, 'we film simultaneously with two lenses, representing the left and right eye, analysing on a monitor what is being shot to ensure that the two images are overlaid in perfect formation for the film to be passed on to post-production.'

Sean works with two hand controls. One adjusts what is called the 'interaxial separation', the distance between the centres of the two camera lenses, which have to relate to the distance between the centre of the human eyes that will be viewing the film, known as the 'interocular separation'. The other control adjusts the 'convergence point', which is where the lenses come together in order to focus on an object or person in a scene so that the viewer gets the impression of depth and distance. By adjusting these two controls it is possible to create a 3D world.

The movie or TV screen is referred to as the Stereo Window and the images projected onto it will appear to be in one of three places: on the screen itself (called zero parallax), behind the screen (positive parallax) or in front of the screen (negative parallax).

RIGHT: *The Orc, Bolg, demonstrates the appearance of 'negative parallax', where an image appears to be in front of the screen.*

Top: *Gandalf prepares to step out of the screen.*
Above: *Lead Stereographer Sean Kelly at work, creating the 'magic' of 3D.*

'Supposing a character is walking towards the screen,' explains Sean, 'and the convergence point is set at, say, twenty feet; if the person walks any closer than that, they will appear to walk out of the screen and come into the audience. That's how the typical 3D gag works but it's not something we want to do all the time, so as our character gets closer to the screen we will adjust the convergence point in order to control their position inside the 3D environment.'

Sean and his colleagues discuss the adjustments they are going to make while the actors are preparing to shoot a scene. 'We watch the rehearsals,' he says, 'finding the perfect settings for the beginning and ending of a shot. By the time they start filming, we have got our moves worked out.'

Scene 133c is currently being rehearsed with Ian McKellen as Gandalf striding towards the camera and speaking. Handing me a pair of 3D glasses and inviting me to watch the monitor, Sean demonstrates how adjusting the interaxial separation and the convergence point can keep Gandalf on the screen (but with a real sense of depth behind him) or gradually edge him out into the negative space between the monitor and my watching eyes. Gandalf's face starts on screen, but first the brim of his wizard's hat and then the tip of his nose and the end of his beard start edging out of the screen until his face is hovering in front of me.

As Sean points out: 'This is probably not an effect that Peter would want to use, though if he asked for a creature to pop up and leap out of the screen that is how we would achieve it. The context is what is important: you could have Gandalf point his staff forward and it could appear to come out into the cinema auditorium, but if he had an important line to say at the same time then the effect might be so distracting that the audience could well miss what he said. We're here to help make a movie; and the movie is about the story not about 3D. We don't want anyone walking out of the cinema saying they didn't know what was going on.'

If the current popularity of 3D is to be anything other than a short-lived fad (as it has been in the past) it has to do more than just create moments that make an audience jump. 'Some people may go to movies looking for a 3D experience,' says Sean, 'but we are trying to change that perception so that people begin to think of it more as a great way of enhancing the storytelling medium. There are always people who will say that they didn't like a 3D film because it wasn't 3D enough or because there was too much 3D; people who want more things coming out of the screen and those who'd rather nothing came out of the screen at all. Hopefully, we'll get to a point where people go to a movie because they want to see that movie and the 3D is just part of what makes it enjoyable.'

Gandalf on 3D

'Once you've seen 3D as expertly shot as these films are,' says Ian McKellen, 'you might find 2D films to be a bit disappointing. In fact, early on in the production, I watched Martin Freeman filming a screen-test where he was walking around as Bilbo. In the foreground, while I was watching him do that, were two screens: one showing how the scene would look in 2D and the other with the 3D version. So I had three options for looking at Bilbo and, I have to tell you – when I put on the special glasses – the one that looked the most believable was the 3D version. *More* believable than actually watching Martin Freeman. More *lifelike* than *life!* Now, *that* is a bit bewildering.'

An Audience with the Great Goblin

'**D**elusional, brutal, totally lacking in empathy and, above all, hideous; he is one of the most unpleasant characters to have ever inhabited the cinema screen.'

The celebrated Australian actor and comedian, Barry Humphries is discussing his portrayal of the Great Goblin, King of Goblin Town in the Misty Mountains where Thorin and the Dwarves are taken prisoner and held captive. 'He is a gigantic and repulsive figure, and yet, one of great charm, dignity and erudition. We realize that, underneath it all, he is probably a New Zealand intellectual, fallen upon hard times.'

Recalling how he came to be involved in the project, Barry says: 'I had a telephone call from someone called Peter Jackson. I was in London, where I sometimes live, and was busy, so I asked him to ring later. Then a penny dropped. I thought, "Could he be related to one of the most gifted people in the entire history of film?" He was and he asked me if I would like to be in his film of *The Hobbit*.'

It was an invitation not to be declined: 'I immediately agreed,' he says, 'for a ridiculously small fee. But the money was not important, it was the opportunity to explore the thing that I like most in life and art: the grotesque. Normality has never interested me. I am drawn to the paranormal, the extraordinary, the bizarre and the outlandish.'

That is certainly borne out by his close association with Dame Edna Everage, housewife, investigative journalist, social anthropologist, talk-show host, swami, spin-doctor, Megastar and Icon, and Sir Les Patterson, Australia's outspoken cultural attaché to the Court of St James's.

For Peter Jackson, having Barry Humphries in the cast was both thrilling and, in anticipation, a source of some apprehension: 'I've been a fan of Barry's for over thirty years,' he says. 'I'd seen Dame Edna's shows in the West End and when she toured New Zealand, but it's always a bit nerve-wracking when you meet people you admire for the first time because you don't want your heroes to disappoint you. Of course, Barry turned out to be everything I'd dreamed he would be: the sweetest, kindest, good-natured, funny man who does really great work.'

For Barry's part, he was understandably keen to know what his character looked like: 'Jackson showed me a little plastic figurine of such ugliness that I really thought it was a part they should get someone else to play: perhaps Dan Aykroyd or possibly Danny DeVito in a fat suit. But they explained that the new techniques would make it possible for me to be extremely large, to begin with, and to conform to the ugliness of the figurine. And I think we've achieved that. People will shrink in horror, but then – to use a modish expression – embrace the character.'

Asked whether he had contributed to the screen realization of the character, Barry says: 'It is *possible* that I made a contribution. Lately, when I've looked in the mirror, I can see that they based it loosely on my own appearance. I've been a little worried, as the years go on – I'm now in the November of my life – by my double chins, which seem to be growing.'

BELOW: *The very great Barry Humphries.* OPPOSITE: *Early conceptual art showing the Goblin King.*

The Goblins' brutally monstrous monarch is not only given voice by Barry Humphries, but was acted out by him in motion-capture, a process which he found both intriguing and baffling: 'You get covered with dots – a sort of white measles suddenly appear all over you – and these, apparently, attract little lasers or beams or something in the camera. If I were a twelve-year-old, I would understand all the technology of this movie, but as I'm not I just go with the flow and enjoy myself.'

The actor was much impressed with the set built for the scenes featuring the Great Goblin: 'The studio was filled with an amazing edifice. Because the Goblin King is a scavenger on a huge scale, his throne room is entirely constructed of rubbish: old timber, terrible skeletons and human remains. It's a forensic paradise. Dwarves are his foe and he is a cannibal, so he's very fond of having them in various culinary experiments. His horrible inner sanctum is filled with the skulls and bones and, sometimes, even the entrails of Dwarves to an extent previously unseen in movies. In fact, I know of no other film where the entrails of Dwarves are examined in such detail, so it's an educational film.'

Of the throne itself, Barry notes: 'There's a hole in the seat, so it is both a throne and also a toilet. The Goblin King is, among other things, grossly incontinent so if he hears the call of nature it doesn't need to interrupt his conversation and, from time to time, a beautifully crafted urn beneath the throne receives a compliment of matter from the Goblin King, generally speaking of ill-digested Dwarf.'

Barry was particularly gratified to discover that the Great Goblin has a song to sing: 'I'm convinced that it will be a huge hit,' he says. 'It will top the charts, as the young folk would express it. It could even go platinum. It is a song of extreme aggression: a hate-filled number, which children will enjoy and senior citizens will appreciate. It's entirely about destruction, death and torture. But I try to do it in a sympathetic way. I've tried, as a matter of fact, to bring out the loveable side of my character – although this attempt has been a total failure.'

Barry is no stranger to musical performance: he was Mr Sowerberry the undertaker in the original 1960 production of *Oliver!* and later played Fagin. However, singing for the Great Goblin proved challenging: 'My character is tone deaf, and so I had to do what is an extremely difficult thing for a person like me, who sings beautifully – I had to sing it *badly*. Having to act and sing badly is difficult for someone who is in the November of his life.'

The Hobbit began life as a children's book, so an obvious question is whether or not it has been translated into a children's film? Barry is adamant: '*The Hobbit* is a film for children in the sense that its scary moments are the scary moments kids enjoy. Some tests have been made on young children, and they have enjoyed it, though they have not slept a wink since and some of them have also developed nervous tics that, apparently, will never go away. Otherwise, yes, it's a children's film, and it is also, not – as is often cornily said – for "the young in heart", but for those who appreciate

'LATELY, WHEN I'VE LOOKED IN THE MIRROR, I CAN SEE THAT THEY BASED IT LOOSELY ON MY OWN APPEARANCE. I'VE BEEN A LITTLE WORRIED, AS THE YEARS GO ON – I'M NOW IN THE NOVEMBER OF MY LIFE – BY MY DOUBLE CHINS, WHICH SEEM TO BE GROWING.'

extravagance and imagination: qualities lacking in almost every movie you ever see these days.'

As a final reflection on his foray into Middle-earth, Barry Humphries says, 'There's much in this film for audiences of all ages, but I think what people will enjoy the most is my appearance as the Great Goblin. Although, as the years pass, you'll forget most of it, my performance will be evergreen in your memory.'

ABOVE: *Once approved, this maquette of the Goblin King in all his glory will be scanned and used as the basis of the 3D animated character.* OPPOSITE: *Kiran is helped into his double-layered Goblin suit. Helping the Goblin extras perform an impromptu song-and-dance number to celebrate the start of location filming.*

Kiran Shah

ASCRIBING CREDIT

'It is surprising how many times you will have seen me on screen without knowing that it's me.' This is no idle boast on the part of Kiran Shah; at 4'1.7" (or 126 cm), he has had a prolific thirty-six year career in the film industry as a scale double and stunt performer on films as diverse as *Star Wars VI – The Return of the Jedi*, *Raiders of the Lost Ark*, *Dark Crystal*, *Baron Munchausen*, *Gothic* and the Superman, James Bond and Harry Potter franchises.

Kiran spent four years in New Zealand working on Peter Jackson's *The Lord of the Rings* trilogy where he doubled for Elijah Wood's Frodo and, at various times, for the other three hobbits.

When he was cast as Ginarrbrik, the White Witch's Dwarf in Disney's *The Lion, the Witch and the Wardrobe* he had a rare opportunity to play a character as himself instead of for someone else.

On returning to New Zealand to work on *The Hobbit: An Unexpected Journey* he learned that he was to have a role of his own as the Scribe of Goblin Town. 'I have been with Peter in his Tolkien world for a long time,' recalls Kiran, 'and I really enjoy what I do. This time, I've had the fantastic additional opportunity to play a character opposite Barry Humphries as the Goblin King, who was lovely and very funny to work with.'

The role as Goblin Scribe required Kiran to wear an animatronic head: 'From the character's features,' he says, 'I was able to decide what mannerisms he would have. However, the head was very heavy and, as the eyes on the mask were above my own, I was completely unable to see anything. Fortunately, having done similar work in the past, I know how to move and where the eye-line ought to be.'

As holder of the Guinness World Record for the 'shortest professional stuntman currently working in film', Kiran's extensive experience saw him through. As Mary Oladapo of Guinness World Records observed when, in 2010, Kiran set a new record as the world's shortest wing-walker: 'Kiran proves that size isn't everything. Even the smallest of people can achieve the greatest of things.'

OVERLEAF: *The Great Goblin on his throne in scale model form surrounded by miniature Dwarves and Goblins* (INSET) *and the real thing in Studio K surrounded by the crew.*

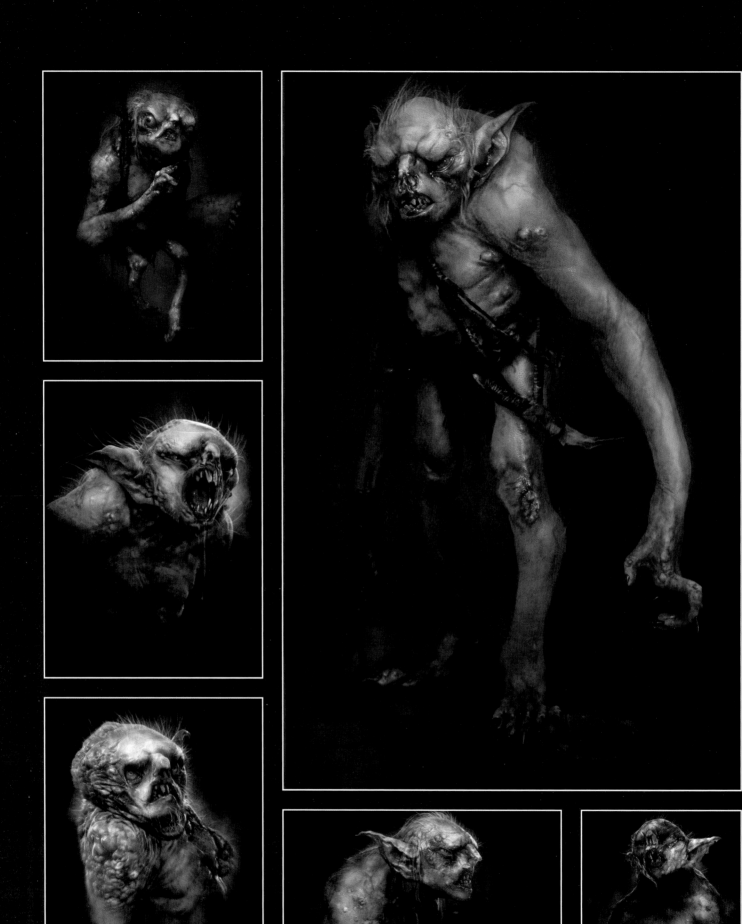

Creating the Goblins

'**G**oblins are cruel, wicked and bad-hearted.' That's how J.R.R. Tolkien described them in *The Hobbit* when Bilbo and the Dwarves find themselves captives of the Goblins living under the Misty Mountains. For Weta Workshop it was an opportunity to bring these unpleasant creatures vividly – and repulsively – to life on screen.

Weta had been working on the process for two years at the point when Peter Jackson replaced Guillermo del Toro as director. 'We were only two months away from the creatures being required on set,' recalls Richard Taylor, 'but we hadn't come up with any designs that captured Peter's imagination. He asked us to picture the Goblins as living underground, grossly deformed and rotting away from every conceivable kind of sickness and disease. So we got to work, desperately aware that we had just eight weeks to get our designs approved, made and on set!'

'THEY ARE RIVETINGLY UGLY AND THE LAST THING YOU WOULD WANT TO SEE IN THE ARMS OF A NURSE IN A MATERNITY WARD.'

After two days of concentrated brainstorming, the Weta team had a new batch of concepts to offer the director. 'They were amazingly grotesque,' says Richard: 'asymmetrical faces, offset eyes, rotting teeth, goitres, hump-backs, legs afflicted with elephantiasis. Anything and everything we could come up with – some of it silly, some of it over the top! Happily, Peter's immediate response was: "This is more like it!"'

Thirty character designs were chosen, but Peter still had some demanding requirements in that he didn't want the Goblins to be made as foam latex body suits of the kind used for the Orcs in *The Lord of the Rings* but wanted to see creatures with bones moving beneath translucent skin.

'We embarked on an intensive research and development phase,' says Richard, 'and found a way of building two suits: one with rigid bones on flexible moving muscles under a second comprising a silicone membrane taken from a sculpture and painted with mottled effects inspired by the skins of axolotls.'

After seven weeks (and, towards the end, several days of total sleep deprivation) Weta Workshop completed thirty full-body suits and heads, ten with animatronic faces, one of which was equipped with full lip-sync capability.

Barry Humphries, who plays the Goblin's King, recalls his response to first seeing his subjects: 'I, who am used to horrible sights, have never seen anything quite so hideous as those Goblins. They are rivetingly ugly and the last thing you would want to see in the arms of a nurse in a maternity ward.'

OPPOSITE: *A ghoulish and ghastly gallery of Goblins! This dark and delicious collection of conceptual designs reveals an array of diseases and deformities.*

Goblins Go to Town

'It is a grungy, vicious, dirty, nasty place – you don't want to be there!' That is Production Designer Dan Hennah's unappealing description of Goblin Town. 'The Goblins are a gruesome gang that live by stealing and looting; they sit around all day indulging in naughty talk then go out at night, filching things and beating up people.'

The process of designing a habitat for these creatures, says Dan, went through various phases before finding the look seen in the film: 'Our conception for Goblin culture was realized when Alan Lee and John Howe came up with drawings showing a giant chasm under the mountain with the Goblins living on a criss-crossing maze of timber gantries and walkways. It is a ramshackle labyrinth where the Goblins swarm around like lice in the seam of your trouser leg.'

RIGHT: *With his 'sword' glowing brightly, Bilbo treads warily through Goblin Town.* BELOW: *John Howe's conceptual painting of Goblin Town.*

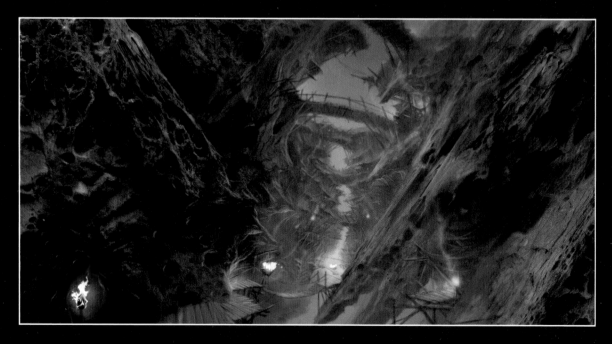

The Quest of Erebor

Friday, 21 October 2011

Everyone at Stone Street Studios is frantically busy preparing for the next day's departure for location shooting. With the second block of filming complete, everyone is conscious of the constantly building media coverage and public anticipation for the eventual arrival of *The Hobbit* in the cinemas of the world.

James Nesbitt is packing and ready to set off with the other Dwarves on the next stage of their journey. It is an opportunity to reflect on the huge project to which they are all committed and with which they will be forever associated: 'This is a story that is ancient,' he says, 'a simple story about heroism and courage, about discovery. There is good and there is great evil in this story, so it is also timeless. Marry that to Peter Jackson's inventiveness and his ability to make that story come alive with heartache and horror, wonder and majesty, and you have a journey that audiences will be eager to follow every step of the way.'

For Elijah Wood, whose return visit to Middle-earth is almost at an end, it is an opportunity to reflect on his experiences in *The Lord of the Rings*: 'I can remember a time when none of us could anticipate how big it was going to be. For us there was a real sense of innocence, of forging new ground, and the only reality was the making of it. I think we all knew that it was going to find an audience and be successful – the anticipation coming from fans of the book was massive. But there was no way of knowing it would so quickly become a staple of popular culture and be regarded as a landmark in cinematic history. It is different for the guys this time around: they are stepping into a world that is established and with a new franchise that has a far greater sense of anticipation as well as a built-in expectation of guaranteed success.'

That is something of which many of those previously involved in *Rings* are all too aware.